George Gardiner Alexander

Lâo-Tsze, the great thinker

with a translation of his thoughts on the nature and manifestations of God

George Gardiner Alexander

Lâo-Tsze, the great thinker
with a translation of his thoughts on the nature and manifestations of God

ISBN/EAN: 9783743657953

Printed in Europe, USA, Canada, Australia, Japan

Cover: Foto ©Raphael Reischuk / pixelio.de

More available books at **www.hansebooks.com**

LÂO-TSZE

THE GREAT THINKER

BY THE SAME AUTHOR.

CONFUCIUS, THE GREAT TEACHER. Crown 8vo, 6s.

Recently Published Oriental Literature.

CHINESE CHARACTERISTICS. By ARTHUR H. SMITH. Second Edition, Revised and Enlarged. Crown 8vo, 10s. 6d.

THE MIND OF MENCIUS; or, Political Economy founded upon Moral Philosophy. A systematic Digest of the Doctrines of the Chinese Philosopher, Mencius. By E. FABER. Post 8vo, 10s. 6d. *Trübner's Oriental Series.*

THE RELIGIOUS SYSTEM OF CHINA: Its Ancient Forms, Evolution, History, and Present Aspect. Manners, Customs, and Social Institutions connected therewith. By J. G. M. DE GROOT. In twelve vols. imp. 8vo, of which two are now out.
Vol. I. The Funeral Rites. Ideas about Resurrection. 12s.
Vol. II. The Grave. 15s.

SHANTUNG. A General Outline of the Geography and History of the Province; a Sketch of its Missions and Notes of a Journey to the Tomb of Confucius. By A. ARMSTRONG. With Map. Royal 8vo, 10s.

LONDON: KEGAN PAUL, TRENCH, TRÜBNER & CO., LTD.

LÂO-TSZE
THE GREAT THINKER

WITH A TRANSLATION OF HIS

THOUGHTS ON THE NATURE AND
MANIFESTATIONS OF GOD

BY

Major-General G. G. ALEXANDER, C.B.

AUTHOR OF "CONFUCIUS, THE GREAT TEACHER"

LONDON

KEGAN PAUL, TRENCH, TRÜBNER & Co., Ltd.

1895

PREFACE.

—-ᴧᴧᴧ—

THE favourable reception given to my work on Confucius has encouraged me to place before the public, in a form which I have thought best adapted to enlist its sympathies, another Chinese classical subject—the life and teaching of the most distinguished of Confucius's contemporaries, Lâo-tsze, the Great Thinker. The great difference between the two men, however, has necessitated, in the present instance, a somewhat modified treatment, inasmuch that whilst the personality of Confucius looms out of the past, a comparatively clear and well-defined shape, that of Lâo-tsze comes down to us so shadowy and indistinct that, apart from a few recorded incidents belonging to his life, our knowledge of him has to be gained from the thoughts to which he gave utterance in his one great work, the Tâo-tĭh-King.

It is for this reason that I have made a translation

of this work, the portion of my task, to which I have devoted the greatest amount of labour, and to which I have made all else subservient. It may be asked why it should be necessary for me to undertake that which has been already accomplished by some of our most eminent Chinese scholars. My answer is, that though the scholastic rendering of such a book may be of the greatest possible value to the student, the philologist, or the man of letters, it is not unfrequently made uninviting, indeed repellent, to the general reader, by a strained literal accuracy which overrides and destroys the interest of the subject. My great endeavour, therefore, has been to steer a middle course between a close verbal line by line translation, and one that in point of breadth falls little short of paraphrase, bearing ever in mind the principles set forth by Dr Legge—our greatest Chinese scholar— who, in the preface to his translation of the Yih-King, which forms the sixteenth volume of the Sacred Books of the East, says :—" The written characters of the Chinese are not representations of words but symbols of ideas, and the combination of them in composition is not a representation of what the writer would say, but of what he thinks. It is vain.

therefore, for a translator to attempt a literal version. When the symbolic characters have brought his mind *en rapport* with that of his author, he is free to render his ideas in his own, or any other speech, in the best manner he can attain to. . . . In the study of a Chinese classical book there is not so much an interpretation of the character employed by the writer as a participation of his thoughts; there is the seeing mind to mind."

But in this view Dr Legge does not stand alone; von Plaenkner, in his German translation of the Tâo-tĭh-King, sets it forth still more forcibly, and though, when putting it into practice, he may have exceeded safe limits, I think there can be but small doubt as to the general soundness of his conclusions.

The mode in which a translation should be carried out is also clearly laid down by Dr Jowett in his preface to the second and third editions of the Dialogues of Plato. He says :—" An English translation ought to be idiomatic and interesting, not only to the scholar but to the unlearned reader. Its object should not simply be to render the words of one language into the words of another, or to preserve the construction and order of the original ; this is the ambition of a schoolboy, who wishes to show that he has made a good use of his dictionary and grammar; but is quite unworthy of the translator who seeks to produce on his reader an impression similar, or nearly similar, to that produced by the original. *To him the feeling should be more important than the exact word"*—the italics are mine. "He should remember Dryden's quaint admonition not to lacquey by the side of his author, but to mount up behind him. He must carry in his mind a comprehensive view of the whole work, of what has preceded, and of what has to follow, as well as of the meaning of particular passages. His version should be based, in the first instance, on an intimate knowledge of the text; but the precise order and arrangement of the words may be left to fade out of sight, when the translation begins to take shape. He must form a general idea of the two languages, and reduce the one to the terms of the other," . . . and more to the same effect.

Strengthened by the opinion of these eminent authorities, I have endeavoured to carry out my work on thoroughly independent lines. My chief aim, and greatest difficulty, has been to find out not so much the exact meaning of the old Philosopher's words as the precise object he had in his mind when using them. I cannot pretend to have succeeded in doing this in all cases, but in no instance have I ventured to give a different reading of the text from that adopted by my predecessors, without having first convinced myself that such a change was absolutely needed, in order to give clearness and comprehensiveness to the ideas which Lâo-tsze was endeavouring to put before the world, and explain with such an earnest vehemence. The difficulties which have to be encountered are indeed very great. In addition to those inherent in the language, are those which proceed from Lâo-tsze having, apparently, written down his thoughts without any systematic plan of arrangement; from the extreme curtness of his style; from his love of thesis and antithesis; his startling paradoxes; quaint illustrations; and now and again incoherences and contradictions.

It may be objected to the phraseology I have adopted that it does not fairly represent the abrupt and rugged style of the original. But I do not consider that this objection can override the fact, that according to the laws of translation already quoted, the more closely the translator approaches to the Chinese text in these particulars, the farther he will be from giving a clear and accurate idea of the spirit and intention, to which the strangely formed sentences of the old Philosopher are but a mere framework. Even in modern languages a strictly verbal and literal translation not only fails to convey a just impression of an author's style, but, frequently, utterly obscures and confuses his meaning. And this becomes accentuated when, as with a language like the Chinese, two or three characters serve to express, or give rise to, such a number of ideas, that they can only be adequately represented by the employment of one or more lengthy English sentences.

But my chief reason for thinking that a new translation of the Tâo-tĭh-King was needed, proceeded from my conviction that all previous renderings of the word "Tâo" were faulty and open to most serious objection; for it is hardly possible to avoid the conclusion that Lâo-tze's great object was to re-establish a belief in the great traditionary First Cause, known and worshipped in primitive times under the name of Tâo; a belief which had gradually become weakened and obscured, until an inferior conception of the Deity had been substituted for it.

I am aware that in having rendered the character, the phonetic form of which is " Tâo," by the word " God ; " instead of leaving it untranslated, as has been done by many previous translators, I have laid myself open to very severe criticism. But it was only after much deep and anxious consideration that I did so. I found that the various substitutes which had been suggested, or, in one or two instances, used, only imperfectly expressed the sense of a character, which apart from the signification attached to it by Lâo-tsze, may be said to have—when taking into account its employment in combination — a greater variety of meanings than that of almost any other character in the Chinese language. Moreover, I was deeply impressed with the insufficiency of the various methods by which the several translators sought to evade or overcome this, their chief diffi-culty, by refusing to employ the single word, which, according to my view, forms the keynote, not only to a portion, but to the whole of Lâo-tzse's thoughts. I fancied I could detect a certain timidity in dealing with this matter, for even those who considered they

had found in the pages of the Tâo-tĭh-King, the
recognition of a triune God, shrank from employing
the one term which would have best enabled them
to enforce their views. This is especially the case
with von Strauss, who, in his able and exhaustive
work on the Tâo-tĭh-King, after having entered fully
into the reasons why the only legitimate rendering of
the character "Tâo" must be "God," still follows
the example of many others and leaves it untranslated. But what he says is so clearly put and so
much to the point that I cannot do better than
reproduce it in his own words. In par. 10, p. xxxiv.
of the introduction to his translation of the Tâo-tĭh-
King, he writes thus :— " Tâo existed as a perfect but
incomprehensible Being, before Heaven and earth
were (chap. 25) — immaterial and immeasurable
(chap. 4),—Invisible and inaudible, mysterious yet
manifest, without shape or form (chap. 14),—super-
sensuous and hidden from our eyes (chaps. 25, 41),—
The eternal foundation of all things (chap. 1), and the
universal progenitor of all beings (chap. 4).—Incapable of being named or defined (chaps. 1, 32), only
capable of being named when revealed by His works
(chaps. 1, 32).—In this dual capacity the source from

which all that is spiritual proceeds (chaps. 1, 6),—for through Him all things have come into existence (chap. 21),—and in like manner all things return again to Him (chap. 16) ;—and it is through Him that this takes place (chap. 40).—Although He is eternal and absolutely free, has no wants or desires (chap. 34),—whilst eternally at rest, is never idle (chap. 37),—Does not grow old (chaps. 30, 55),—Is omnipresent, immutable, and self-determined (chap. 35),—Creates, preserves, perfects, nourishes, and protects, all things ; hence is glorified for His beneficence, and held in high honour (chap. 51),—for He loves all things and does not act as a mere ruler (chap. 34) —even as though He were powerless (chap. 14).— The spirituality of His nature not to be doubted (chap. 21),—though He only reveals Himself to those who are free from all desires (chap. 1).—He who regulates his actions by Him will become one with Him (chap. 23),—Therefore He is the foundation of the highest morality (chap. 38).—He it is who bestows, and makes perfect (chap. 41),—and gives peace (chap. 46),—Is the universal refuge, the good man's treasure, the bad man's deliverer, and the pardoner of guilt (chap. 62).

"We believe that any impartial person who might be asked, what word in our language would best apply to the Being of whom all this can be said, would be compelled to answer, ' by the word God, and by none other!' And how can anyone with a knowledge of the foregoing evidence have the slightest doubt of Lâo-tsze having possessed, in a remarkable degree, a great and deep consciousness of God of so sublime and precise a nature, that it almost realises the idea of God belonging to Revelation, though it is needless to remark that the latter greatly surpasses it in the profundity and fulness of its manifestations. But in all the centuries preceding the Christian era, no similar revelation was made beyond the one made to Israel."*

* " Tâo war, als unbegreiflich vollkommenes Wesen, vor Entstehung Himmels und der Erde (Kap. 25). Körperlos und unermesslich (Kap. 4), unsichtbar und unhörbar, geheimnissvoll und kundlich, gestaltlos und bildlos (Kap. 14), übersinnlich und verborgen (Kap. 25, 41), ist er der ewige Urgrund von allem (Kap. 1) und aller Wesen Urvater (Kap. 4) ; als solcher aber unaussprechlich und unnennbar (Kap. 1, 32), nennbar nur als durch die Schöpfung Offenbarter (Kap. 1, 32) und in dieser, Duplicität alles Geistigen Ausgang (Kap. 1, 6). Denn durch Ihn ist Alles entsprungen (Kap. 21), Alles kehrt auch wieder zu Ihm zurück (Kap. 16), und es zu sich wieder zurückzubringen, ist sein Thun (Kap. 40) ; denn obwol ewig ohne Verlangen oder Bedürfniss (Kap. 34), und daher ewig ohne Thun, is ter doch nie unthätig (Kap. 37), da er, nie alternd (Kap. 30, 35), allgegenwärtig, selbst unwandelbar und nur sich

But von Strauss does not stand alone. In the
introduction to a translation of the Tâo-tĭh-King by
the Rev. John Chalmers, A.M., the author, after
having passed in review the several English words
which might be substituted for the Chinese character
Tâo, gives as his reason for leaving it untranslated,
his belief that no one of them can be considered an
exact equivalent; and then he proceeds to say: "I
would translate it by 'the Word' in the sense of 'the

selbst bestimmend (Kap. 25), alle Wesen erschafft, erhält, gestaltet,
vollendet, nähret und schirmet, die deshalb alle Ihn ehren und seine
Wohlthat preisen (Kap. 51), weil er sie alle liebt und keines Herrscher
ist (Kap. 34), gleich als wäre er machtlos (Kap. 40). In ihm ist Geist,
und sein Geist ist das Zuverlässigste (Kap. 21), aber nur der Begier-
delose erschauet ihn (Kap. 1). Wer sein Thun nach Tâo bestimmt,
der wird eins mit Ihm (Kap. 23); Tâo ist daher auch der Grund
höchster Sittlichkeit (Kap. 38). Er ist der grosse Geber, Vollender
(Kap. 41) und Friedebringer (Kap. 46); aller Wesen Zuflucht, der
Guten Schatz, der Nichtguten Retter, und der da Schuld vergiebt
(Kap. 62).

" Wir meinen, jeder Unbefangene, den man fragte, wie man in unserer
Sprache das Wesen bezeichne, vom dem diess Alles ausgesagt werden
könne, musste antworten : Gott, und nur Gott ! Und wer die vorstehen-
den Aussagen zusammen fasst, dem kann gar kein Zweifel bleiben, dass
Lâo-tsze ein überraschend grosses und tiefes Gottbewusstseyn, einen
erhabenen und sehr bestimmten Gottesbegriff gehabt habe, der sich
fast durchgängig mit dem Gottesbegriff der Offenbarung deckt, sofern
dieser nicht über ihn hinaus tiefer und reicher entwickelt ist was dem
allerdings keiner Nachweisung bedarf. Aber ausserhalb Israels wird
aus allen vorchristlichen Jahrhunderten nichts Aehnliches nachzuweisen
seyn."

b

Logos,' but this would be like settling the question which I wish to leave open, viz.:—what amount of resemblance there is between the Logos of the New Testament and this Tâo, which is its nearest representative in Chinese? In our version of the New Testament in Chinese we have in the first chapter of St John—' In the beginning was Tâo,' &c."

It surely must be conceded, that this evasion of a great difficulty, by either retaining the untranslated Chinese word Tâo in the English text, or by so rendering it as to destroy and confuse the harmony of the arguments put forward by Lâo-tsze, can have no other effect than to make it almost impossible to understand, or to form a just appreciation of, a book which has been characterised by a distinguished oriental scholar,[*] as :—" One of the most eminent masterpieces of the Chinese language, one of the profoundest philosophical books the world has ever produced, and one the authenticity of which has been least contested in his fatherland, and even in the circle of European Sinologues."

Fortified by such opinions as those I have placed

---

[*] G. v. der Gabelenz, Professor of Eastern Asiatic Languages at the University of Leipsic. In the *China Review*, vol. xvii. No. 4.

before the reader, my chief endeavour has been, to restore to the writings of the old philosopher, what I conceive to be their real philosophical and meta-physical value; at the same time, it has to be re-membered, that the belief in a great traditional First Cause, which he was endeavouring to re-establish, was founded on a purely abstract idea of an overruling deity, and we must refrain as much as possible from seeking to bring it into harmony with the idea of God which belongs to our own beliefs.

Although the Tâo-tïh-King necessarily forms the central point in connection with Lâo-tsze and his opinions, I have thought it desirable—indeed indis-pensable—to enter at some length, in the preliminary chapters, on all those antecedent causes, which were the chief factors in producing the religious and philosophical views entertained by the great Chinese idealist. Without some such introductory matter, neither the man nor his thoughts could be rightly understood, and my chief object throughout has been to popularise, as far as possible, the thoughts of a great thinker in a far distant age.

It will be seen that the writings of Lâo-tsze's fol-lowers, and the subsequent development which his doctrines—so terribly to their detriment—received at their hands, have not formed part of the plan to the execution of which I have confined myself. Had I done so, I should have been unable to place the venerable philosopher before the reader, in the light of his own pure thoughts, for they would have been obscured and blurred by the misconstruction put upon them by his ignorant and superstitious adherents. I have, for the same reason, accepted as seldom as possible the readings of his numerous Chinese commentators; for, whether they came from members of the Tâoist school, or from the disciples of Confucius, I have invariably found that Lâo-tsze's views were dealt with from the standpoint of their own sectarian proclivities, and brought down, as far as possible, to the level of their own shallow capacities.

The division of the Tâo-tĭh-King into chapters, was not the work of Lâo-tsze. It was a subsequent arrangement, often carried out in such a manner as to disturb the sequence and completeness of the writer's arguments and method of demonstration. I have, however, with a view to facility of reference, followed the usual course, and retained them, though I have discarded the titles attached to the several chapters, for they also did not belong to the original work, and are often very misleading.

Whilst making myself acquainted with the various translations of the Tâo-tîh-King, I have confined myself, for the purposes of comparison—as will be seen in the Appendix—to those of Dr Legge, Victor von Strauss, and Stanislas Julien, and in most cases when I have found myself in non-agreement with those eminent authorities, and unable to modify my views, I have given my reasons for adhering to them.

Of course it would have been preferable to have made use of Chinese characters in the Appendix instead of their phonetic equivalents, but the great expense attending such an arrangement made me reluctant to adopt it.

CONTENTS.

—◆◇◆—

PART I.

ORIGINS AND ANTECEDENTS

ORIGINS AND ANTECEDENTS.

IT is probable that no one age of which we have
any knowledge could be characterised as utterly
deficient in Great Thinkers, for the term is, after
all, only a relative one; and it may be assumed that
the further we go back—provided a certain stage
of civilisation has been reached—the more prominently they would stand out from their fellows.
The number, too, of such men must at first have
been extremely small, and it is doubtless to this
cause, as much as to their intellectual superiority,
that they were able to produce such a profound
impression upon their contemporaries, and not unfrequently such a widespread and long continued
influence upon succeeding generations.

It must not be forgotten, however, that the
largest proportion of those great thoughts which
were the chief factors in moulding man's destinies
have remained unrecorded, so that it is only now
and again that the individual intelligence of the
Present can be directly brought into close and

sympathetic contact with the thoughts and feelings possessed by some one person in the distant
Past.

Possibly, if a History of Human Thought were
to be written, we should be compelled to acknow-
ledge that the mental activity of mankind is
somewhat fitful in its action, and that, at times, it
seems to ebb and flow like the waters of the ocean,
now gathering its forces together in monstrous and
irresistible waves, and then, as if exhausted by
its fierce energy, showing an unruffled surface for
such a long period, as to make it difficult to believe that those forces were still there, and would,
before long, be again in violent and antagonistic
motion.

Just as the waters of the ocean would become
putrid but for the revivifying power of its currents
and its storms, so would mankind have remained
a mere inert, unprogressive mass, so low down in
the social scale that there would be little to distinguish them from the lower animals, had it not
been for the agitation produced by the influence
of its exceptional thinkers.   It was through the
struggle of these to set themselves free from the
shackles of degrading prejudices and beliefs that
their fellows became emancipated from a state of
bondage, against which they had   otherwise,   so

strong is the force of habit, made no protest ; and yet, how strange it is!—often when in the very act of striking off our old fetters we are unwittingly forging new ones, which in due time will have to be dealt with by a fresh set of thoughts, which in the end will probably be productive of similar results.

In the sixth, fifth, and fourth centuries preceding our era, the nations of the Eastern world were singularly rich in Great Thinkers, and amongst them was one who has a greater claim upon our notice than he has hitherto received—I speak of the writer upon "The Nature and Attributes of God"—Lâo-tsze the Chinese.

The subject is a very difficult one. It would be vain to deny that, as a rule, the public are not easily induced to take an active or sympathetic interest in anything which may belong to the history or the social conditions of the strange and comparatively isolated people who have occupied, for so many thousand years, such a large portion of the far East. Yet it would be useless for me to try and convey an accurate idea of the man, or of the thoughts to which he gave expression, unless I could at the same time enable the reader to possess a sufficient comprehension of the antecedent causes and conditions which placed the peculiar stamp characteristic of the Chinese race upon the Thinker, and led him to adopt and promulgate ideas which he professed to have derived from the beliefs prevalent in primeval times, before, as he thought, man's original perfection had been vitiated by a prolonged contact with the world.   Confucius had equally drawn his inspirations from the Past, but, according to Lâo-tsze, he had not gone back far enough, and hence the narrowness and insufficiency of his views ; this not said in so many words, but expressed more or less indirectly in almost every page of his writings, as will be seen by-and-bye.

I have commenced by speaking of Lâo-tsze as " The Chinese," and this brings us at once face to face with a series of questions, the answering of which has caused a considerable amount of controversy and vexation of spirit :—What is the origin of the Chinese as a people ?   Whence did they obtain their social and political organisation ? From what sources, extraneous to themselves, did they gain a knowledge of the sciences, and the foundations upon which they constructed their written character ?   Wherefore is it that in their early civilisation so much is to be found which would seem to have a Babylonian origin ?—with many others of a similar nature ; all somewhat perplexing, and none as yet capable of such a solution as would render all further investigation superfluous.

Such being the case, I shall not attempt to answer these questions categorically, or to analyse the arguments by which the various theories respecting them are sought to be established, but confine myself, as far as possible, to placing before the reader such conclusions as I have been led to arrive at, after the most careful consideration of all the circumstances connected with the first establishment of the Chinese in the basin of the Yellow River, and the causes which most probably enabled them to obtain such a marked superiority, both morally and physically, over their neighbours.

If the reader will refer to a map of that portion of the Chinese Empire known as China Proper, he will see that it is enclosed between the sea on its east and south, and vast ranges of mountains on its west and north. From these main ranges other minor ones project in various directions, and from these again innumerable spurs are thrown out, of greater or lesser altitude, which spread over a vast portion of the interior, so that China, instead of being one great plain, as it is popularly supposed to be, is in point of fact a very mountainous country, only accessible to the outer world by means of a few difficult mountain passes and desert routes, or by the sea.

Intersected by many rivers, two of them, having their sources not far from each other in the mountains of Thibet, flow throughout the land in widely deviating courses. The northernmost of these two rivers is the Yellow River, or Hwang-ho; the southernmost is the Yang-tsze Kiang. The former has a length of 2600 miles, the latter of 3300, but notwithstanding this difference, the area of their basins is nearly equal, that of the Yellow River being 540,000 square miles, which is only 8000 less than that of the Yang-tsze Kiang. Until some forty years ago both rivers discharged themselves, within a short distance of each other, into the Yellow Sea, which received its name from the discoloration occasioned by their waters; but then the Yellow River, for the ninth recorded time, once more changed its direction, and returning to an ancient channel, forced its way through the alluvial plains it had done so much to form, until it reached the long deserted shore of the Gulf of Pĕche-li.

It is to this river, often spoken of as " China's sorrow," that, for reasons which will presently appear, I particularly wish to direct the reader's attention, for it is in its basin—which may be regarded as the cradle of the Chinese as a nation—that history first brings them under our notice ; but the earliest annals give us no information whatever with respect to their origin, nor of the circumstances which led to their settlement in those regions. If, however, the very widely accepted view be true, that the earliest immigrants came from the north-west, and the physical conditions of the country through which they had to pass were much the same as they are now—and of this we have no positive knowledge—

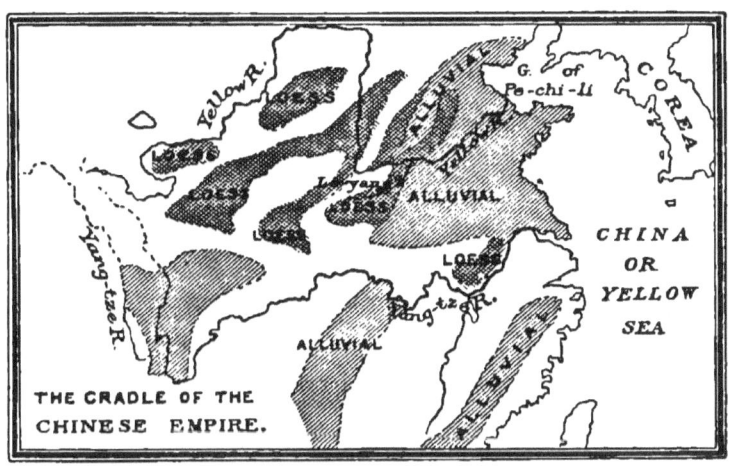

THE CRADLE OF THE CHINESE EMPIRE.

it is tolerably certain they must have advanced by a route which would have led them to strike the Yellow River somewhere in that portion of its course where its current trends to the north. In search, probably, of a milder clime and a more fruitful soil than that of the home they had deserted, they would naturally continue to move on in the direction of the

south, when, after having effected their passage of
the river, impassable mountains would bar their
farther progress in that direction, and compel them
to turn to the east. Moving slowly on, and occupy-
ing the country as they went, this course would
eventually bring them once more to the banks of
the Yellow River, at that point where its stream turns
for the last time its direction towards the east and
becomes the great fertiliser of the plains. Here the
wanderers, finding all their hopes realised—for this
region has ever been regarded as the garden of China
—would naturally establish themselves permanently,
and in the course of a long period of time, the
duration of which we can form no estimate, lay down
the foundations of a civilised state whilst gradually
obtaining a preponderating influence over their less
favoured neighbours.

Even had the route of the first immigrants led
them at the commencement of their wanderings
farther to the east, the only difference would have
been, that by descending the eastern banks of the
Yellow River to the same point, a change in the order
of distribution might have been effected, without
producing any alteration in subsequent events.

As has been already said, the region which thus
became the cradle of the Chinese Empire, and which
includes the modern provinces of Shen-si, Shan-si,

and Ho-nan, is called the Garden of China ; and this is mainly attributable to the fact that it has the special advantage of possessing over a considerable portion of its area, as will be seen by a reference to the sketch map on a former page, a deep, rich, fertilising, yellow loam—the " loess "—which, under the influence of a favourable climate, is productive of an extraordinary luxuriance of vegetable growth. In addition to this, the mountains are rich in minerals, and the hill-sides covered with wild mulberry trees, the leaves of which supply food for the innumerable caterpillars whose silken filaments are known to have been utilised at a very early period, and woven into fabrics which in the course of time became famous throughout the world.

The alluvial plains through which the lower Yellow River takes its course are also extremely fertile, but at the very commencement of the historical period, we find enormous difficulties connected with drainage, and the regulation of the water-ways, had to be over-come ; and it was probably in the struggles which they gave rise to, that the early settlers con-tracted those laborious and industrious habits, by which the Chinese have always been so greatly distinguished.

It is only reasonable to conclude, that the excep-tional advantages enjoyed by the Chinese in the basin of the Yellow River, assisted their development in much the same way as somewhat similar conditions had so marvellously forwarded that of the settlers on the banks of the Euphrates and the Nile; and it is difficult to see why, from the beginning, their progress towards civilisation should not have been a natural process, mainly produced by the circumstances in which they were placed, rather than an artificial growth, owing its existence almost entirely to external influences. .

The distribution of land and water some five or six thousand years ago in Asia, was certainly very different to what it is now. The intercourse between peoples separated by great distances could not have been easy or frequent, and of course with regard to the prehistoric times, we have no knowledge whatever respecting it; it is evident, however, that the position of the dwellers in the basin of the Yellow River, must have given them superior facilities for communicating with the outside world, to those possessed by the tribes spread over the other parts of China, and it is extremely probable that they may, through this medium, have obtained some knowledge of the advanced culture of the West, even before the advent of the Bac tribe or tribes, which is said to have taken place somewhere about the twenty-third century B.C.

According to several eminent modern authorities, it is to the arrival of these tribes from the confines of Elam, that we have to look not only for the first establishment of the Chinese as a people, and as a nation, but for the introduction of a culture gained from Babylonian sources, which was to exercise such a remarkable effect upon the ·destinies of the empire of which they were the founders.

This view is principally based upon the circumstance of certain affinities having been discovered to exist, between the earliest Akkadian writing and the most ancient written characters of the Chinese ; upon the close resemblance of scientific formularies and social methods, adopted by the Chinese, to those of the Babylonians ; and upon many minor details, which, however important in the aggregate, require a degree of individual attention quite beyond what it is in my power to give them in these pages.

I have gone, most carefully, over all that has been written upon this subject, but after having done so I am bound to confess I consider the conclusions which have been arrived at as premature. The investigations which have led to them are of the greatest possible value, but at present they cannot be said to have reached a point which would justify any definite decision being arrived at with respect

to them.* In Ethnological questions, as indeed with
all other questions, there is nothing so likely to lead
us into error as reasoning from analogy, or allowing
ourselves to build up our theories on resemblances
or even isolated coincidences. For example, the cir-
cumnavigator, Cook, discovered on the north-western
coast of America an Indian tribe who sought to
adorn themselves by a most painful perforation of
the lower lips, into which they inserted some circular
ornament so as to make it protrude in the most
disgusting manner ; and in recent years a negro tribe
in Central Africa were found to have adopted an
identical method for beautifying their persons. In
each case the custom was an entirely isolated one, and
there could have been no possible connection between
the two peoples.

But it is difficult to understand what effect the
arrival of the Bacs could have produced upon the
people already in possession of the land they
coveted, unless we are able to form an approxi-
mate idea of their numbers, and of the proportion
in which they stood to those they had either to
conquer or displace. That the numbers on one
side or the other must have been very great is

* Since this was written the lamented death of Professor Terrien de
Lacouperie, one of the most zealous and indefatigable oriental scholars
of the day, who was the leading advocate of this view, has created a
void which will not be easily filled up.

evident, for from the oldest Chinese records which are acknowledged to be authentic, we learn that great works of drainage and reclamation were being carried on at the time which is fixed for the arrival of the Bacs, and such a vast undertaking could only have been conducted by a government, capable of exercising a controlling power over an immense body of workers, withdrawn from the exercise of their ordinary avocations.

Then comes in the question of race, for however valuable Philology and Archæology may be, they are insufficient of themselves to settle the difficulties belonging to origins, and in all matters connected with Ethnology, physical agencies must always hold a high place. For although it may be true that affinities in language, and a close resemblance in customs and modes of thought, cannot be neglected, they must be combined with a study of the anatomical divergences which set their special stamp upon portions of the human race, and thus enable us to classify and arrange what would otherwise remain hopelessly confused.

And this brings me to a point, which, considering its important bearing upon all that concerns the origin and evolution of the Chinese, has been strangely overlooked: I refer to the peculiar conformation of the eyelids, which is spoken of in all Ethnological works as "the Mongolian eye."

The questions to be settled respecting it, are whether this remarkable racial peculiarity was shared by the immigrating Bac tribes, or strictly confined to the earlier dwellers in the basin of the Yellow River, by whom it was transmitted to their descendants? Or was it common or universal amongst those tribes subsequently absorbed or displaced on the extension of the empire? Surely these are subjects worthy of serious consideration, and inasmuch as representatives of those early inhabitants of China, most frequently spoken of as aboriginal, still exist, living under conditions of independence and seclusion, which would preserve them to a large extent from admixture with their neighbours, there could in their case be no great difficulty in obtaining the amount of information suitable to our purpose. But it is singular how little the meaning, of what is commonly referred to as the "Mongolian eye," is understood. I had searched in vain for a clear and accurate definition of it, when I came across a work by Dr. Erwin Baelz, published at Yokohama in 1883, entitled "Die Körperlichen Eigenschaften des Japaner," in which I found it minutely described, and to that work I would refer the reader who might wish to obtain a thorough knowledge of the subject. But without entering too fully into it, I would observe that the commonly entertained idea, respecting the exceptional appearance of the Chinese eye being entirely due to a certain obliquity of position, is erroneous ; for this seeming obliquity is nothing more than the effect produced by the abnormal structure of the eyelids consequent on the small elevation of the nasal bones, which causes the epicanthus, or fold of skin covering the inner canthus of the eye, to be tightly drawn down in an oblique fold, so as to completely hide the small portion of red tissue—the caruncula lachrymalis—which in the eyes of most other races is so much in evidence. In addition to this the orbital furrow or hollow under the eyebrows is all but absent, in consequence of the non-projection of the frontal bones of the forehead, which is in most cases nearly flat ; and it is hardly possible to doubt that the general effect produced by these several structural divergencies from the normal type, would of themselves be sufficient to give those who possessed them, a claim to being considered a distinct family irrespective of any other physical peculiarities by which the Mongolian race may be distinguished.

When we come to deal with the origin of the Chinese from the point of view of language, we

B

are again confronted with difficulties it is not easy
to surmount. But at least this is known—the
structure of the Chinese language, from its paucity
of vocables, its early monosyllabic form, and the
total absence of those changes of the words themselves in combination, which are regulated by
certain rules and principles, known to us as grammar,
tends to prove its close affinity to those primitive
forms of speech in which man first sought to
communicate his wants and feelings. And when
we study the written character, the same conviction
is forced upon us, for when traced backwards from
the symbolic to what may be called the pictorial
stage, it is found to have a close resemblance, indeed
in many cases an absolute coincidence, with both
the earliest Akkadian and Egyptian forms of
writing. The natural conclusion to be drawn from
this is, that these three written languages must
have been derived from a common source; and
although I know that this view has been contested,
the data upon which it has been sought to establish
the opposing theories still presents itself to my
mind as inconclusive and incomplete.

There is one peculiarity belonging to the Chinese
language which is absent from all others. Whilst
the Akkadians and Egyptians gradually transformed
their hieroglyphic and symbolic characters into

phonetic signs having a syllabaric or alphabetic value, the Chinese, after making a certain progress in the same direction, the traces of which are still apparent, seemed suddenly to have stopped short, and then to have devoted all their energies to enlarging and perfecting the remarkable ideographic system, which forms such a striking monument of human ingenuity, and which perhaps has done more to preserve their nationality and keep them together as a separate people, than any other method that could have been devised.

The area over which this language was spread in prehistoric times has yet to be ascertained, for we do not even know if it were the one spoken and introduced by the Bacs, or if it were confined, at first, to the inhabitants of the basin of the Yellow River, or whether it was also in use amongst the various tribes spread over the more southerly portions of the Eastern Continent.

It is true that evidence exists of certain tribes, who dwelt outside the borders of the states then comprising the Chinese Empire, speaking a language so different from that of the people who subsequently subdued them, that they could only be communicated with through interpreters, but this does not throw very much light upon the subject, for even now in China the vernacular spoken in the different pro-

vinces varies so greatly, that it may be possible
to hear—as I have done—two Chinese conversing
together in "pidgin" English or Malay, through
being quite incapable of communicating with each
other in their own language.

Besides, when we take into consideration the vast
extent of territory occupied by scattered settlements,
often widely separated from each other, and almost
isolated through the want of roads and facilities for
communication, it would be strange if, in the course
of time, an originally common language had not
become transformed into a number of dialects, differ-
ing widely from each other; and this would be the
more certain to take place amongst peoples who had
no literature to form a fixed standard. We have a
striking example of the way in which new languages
are developed, in the great variety of tongues which
arose in Europe in the course of a very few centuries
after the fall of the Roman Empire, amongst the
races having a common origin and a cognate form of
speech. But perhaps the most striking instance of
the rapid modifications which may take place after
the separation of a people, is that afforded by the
Iroquois. Belonging to the same race, and speaking
the same tongue, on the removal of the several tribes
to localities separated by no great distances, and
almost in touch with each other, so speedily did this

change take place, that in the course of a very short period of time they became perfectly unintelligible to one another, so much so, that on their reunion in later days it became necessary for them to decide upon which of the dialects, or new languages, should be accepted as the general medium of communication.

To sum up, the conclusions I have arrived at, with respect to the origin of the Chinese, are :—That an immense period of time must have elapsed between the period of their first appearance in the basin of the Yellow River, and the date at which they are first brought under our notice in the pages of the Shoo-king ; that from the superior physical conditions of the territory in which they were located, their social and political progress could not fail to be more rapid than that of their less favoured neighbours ; that both their written and spoken language exhibit signs of having been directly derived from a primitive and original source ; and that, at the advent of the Bacs, upon which so much stress has been laid, said to have taken place about the time when their history begins, they must, as well in numbers as in organisation, have reached a point which would have rendered them capable of assimilating—whether as an independent or a conquered people—whatever knowledge which might have been introduced amongst them, outside of that which they had previously been able to arrive at.

I think where we fail most in the consideration of these questions, is in not being able sufficiently to realise the enormous periods of time, extending far beyond the reach of all historical research, required to transform families and tribes into organised political societies, such in point of fact as the one the Chinese had attained to, when history first brings them under our notice. Neither can the habit of industry, which alone enables a man to become a successful cultivator of the soil, be rapidly formed, and it was then, as now, possessed by the Chinese in a very remarkable degree. The character of a people requires time for its development, and certainly that of the first dwellers on the banks of the Yellow River, can hardly be said to have been immature.

When we come to the consideration of the social and political condition of the Chinese at the commencement of their history, together with its subsequent development, we rapidly begin to feel that we are standing on surer ground.

For all that concerns the dawn of Chinese history, a more reliable authority can scarcely be found than the accounts which are presented to us in the pages of the Shoo-king. Unfortunately they are only fragmentary, being but a portion of extracts made by

Confucius from the voluminous official records, which were hopelessly lost in the general destruction of all historical books and documents ordered by the first autocratic ruler of China in the second century B.C. The Shoo-king was only saved from the same fate by a mere accident, nor was it found possible to restore it to its original completeness.

What had made the destruction of all historical records comparatively easy of accomplishment, was the circumstance of their being preserved as State papers, under the special care of officers appointed for that purpose, not only at the Imperial Court but at the Courts of the several feudal States, and it is through the writings of Confucius having had a separate and independent existence, that their re-covery was made possible.

The opening chapter of the Shoo - king com-mences at a period which is set down as 2356 B.C. We are at once introduced to a settled form of monarchical government, busily occupied in vast works of drainage and reclamation, for the Yellow River was then, as it has frequently been since, ex-tremely troublesome, and no small amount of skill and labour was required to bring its turbulent waters into subjection. But apart from these physical operations, we have accounts of reforms and regula-tions connected with a great variety of subjects

bearing on social and political progress. Amongst
these may be enumerated laws for the establishment
of harmony amongst the people. The arrangement of
the calendar on an astronomical basis, and the proper
division of the seasons; the establishment of fixed
boundaries between the several States; the settlement
of the land tenures; the creation of various grades of
a feudal nobility, with their distinctive dresses and
insignia; the ordering of the sacrificial rites, and the
selection of localities for their celebration; the establishment of a musical scale in accordance with the
sounds produced from twelve tubes of a fixed length
and diameter, which tubes were also made to serve as
standards for length and capacity; the construction
of a criminal code; methods for placing a fair valua-
tion on the land, and for raising a revenue; and the
establishment of a currency, specimens of which still
exist. And all this, with much more, dealt with in
a period of a few hundred years.

The sovereigns of this period were put forward,
some eighteen hundred years later, by Confucius as
the only models worthy of imitation. Its criminal
code formed the basis upon which all later ones
were constructed. And its social and political forms
are, in a modified degree, those upon which the
organisations of Society and the State may be said
to rest at the present day.

Even then, a high degree of manufacturing skill had been reached, for the early Chinese were skilful weavers both of silken and linen fabrics; and they were able to apply the metals, of which their mountains gave them an abundant supply, not only to useful but to ornamental purposes, and a copper currency had been established, of which specimens exist dating back to between 3000 and 2000 years B.C. But in public estimation, of all the useful arts, agriculture held the highest place. And as the produce of the land formed the chief source of revenue, no efforts were spared to make it as productive as possible. The taxes were levied on a system by which their amount was regulated in accordance with the natural fertility, or poverty, of the soil; the whole country being surveyed and the land classified, for revenue purposes. The whole territory was at first divided into nine districts, of which the domain of the supreme ruler formed the nucleus, each district being governed by an officer whose title had the meaning of pastor or shepherd, but in the course of a few years these districts became converted into all but independent States, ruled over by hereditary chiefs who not infrequently assumed the title of kings, whilst accepting the position of feudatories, to at first an elective, but subsequently an hereditary sovereign, whose authority outside his own State gradually became extremely small, though certain religious and ceremonial functions were relegated to him which he alone was capable of performing.

The extension of the Empire must have been rapid, for in the reign of the second Emperor mentioned in the Shoo-king, the number of districts were increased to twelve, and included in their limits nearly all that part of modern China between the Yang-tsze Kiang and the great wall. And this naturally gave to the Chinese all the advantages to be derived from the fruitful "loess" deposits and the rich alluvial plains. The possession of this vast territory was not obtained without resistance on the part of the tribes who, on account of their long occupation, had established rights they were determined to defend ; but after a severe struggle they were either reduced to subjection or compelled to take refuge in mountain fastnesses, from which for some time it was found impossible to expel them, and their descendants have in a few instances preserved a certain amount of isolation and independence to the present day.

Even at this early period of Chinese history, a condition of civilisation had been reached very different from that belonging to the traditional times, when the skins of wild animals formed the only wear, and no other means for recording events existed than that afforded by knotted cords. The reign of law had been established ; and although the criminal code contained enactments which do not accord with our latter-day's idea of justice, they bear evidence of having been carefully thought out ; and however harsh and cruel it may seem that the punishment for an offence should be extended to the criminal's family, we must not forget, that it was only late in the 17th century that a similar law was abrogated in Russia.

The early religion of the Chinese had long passed out of those phases of superstition in which material forms are made to do duty as deities, whose cruel anger can only be appeased by human sacrifices. Of these latter, however, a tradition still remained. And the practice, which was at the time all but universal throughout the other portions of the globe, was long continued by the Scythians and the various Tartar tribes inhabiting the northern frontiers, in whose case it had assumed the form of immolating victims on the death of their chiefs or great men. There is, too, undoubted evidence of such a custom having been practised by the Chinese, for isolated cases of it appear down to a comparatively late period. That this, however, was exceptional, is shown by the very early substitution of a block of wood as a representative of the living man ; whilst, in order to avoid the destruction of useful and valuable property at the burial of their friends, they adopted a system—which holds at the present day—of burning a quantity of paper counterfeits, which they destroyed with a liberality proportionate to the amount of wealth the deceased possessed and the veneration in which he was held. At the same time, self-immolation at the tomb of a relative has always been, and still is, held in high honour, and number-less arches have been erected to commemorate the virtues of wives who thus put an end to their lives on the death of their husbands.

It is indeed generally allowed, that the early beliefs of the Chinese were more spiritual in their nature than those of any other primitive people with whom we are acquainted. Throughout their classical writings traces are to be found of the recognition of an overruling First Cause, known under different names, such as " Heaven," or the " Almighty Ruler," or by a term which I have translated " God." A Power which dominated over the conceptions of a Pantheism which fur-nished every locality with a presiding Genius or Spirit, to whom worship had to be paid in a mountain set apart for that purpose. The choice of these mountains being one of the first acts an Emperor was called upon to perform, on the creation of a new district.

There was no priesthood. It was the duty of the Emperor—for so it is most convenient to designate the head of the state—to perform the sacrificial rights by which the favour of High Heaven was besought on behalf of the Empire as a whole: the Rulers of the several districts or states, being in like manner the intercessors for that portion of it over which their authority extended ; whilst the heads of families were restricted to the ceremonies which had for their object the welfare of their children and the members of their own households.

Such is a brief summary of what is revealed to us in the opening chapters of Chinese history. Subsequently a slow but steady progress was continued on the same lines: the written language was modified and developed ; a literature gradually formed ; the organisation of the several states, into which the original districts had been converted, perfected ; the limits of the empire extended ; and large bodies of men trained to arms, ostensibly for feudal service, but more frequently in order that they might be employed in internecine wars between rival vassal states, or in resisting some unwelcome demand proceeding from their Liege Lord. For the machinery of state did not always work smoothly, and there were times when it seemed as if the vast fabric it had taken so much time and labour to create, would be torn to pieces in the protracted and bloody wars caused by the rivalry of tyrannical and ambitious princes.

The abridgement of the authority which had belonged to the first sovereigns was mainly due to the vices and incapacity of their successors. But although the power of these had become so diminished, that outside their own states it was little more than nominal, and that their misconduct had twice led to their deposition and a change of dynasty, the federation of the several states under the headship of an hereditary ruler continued to be the recognised principle upon which the empire was organised for more than two thousand years; when, three centuries later than the time in which Lâo-tsze lived, the semi-independence of the states was destroyed, and the whole empire united under the rule of a sovereign, who assumed autocratic powers, and inaugurated the new regime by a wholesale destruction of the State records, and all works bearing upon the history of the past—hopelessly lost treasures which succeeding generations sought in vain to recover.

Some five hundred years before Lâo-tsze lived, Woo-wang, one of China's greatest heroes, had hurled the cruel and licentious tyrant, who was the last sovereign of a dynasty which had lasted more than six hundred years, off his throne, and placing himself upon it, became the founder of a dynasty which, after the name of his patrimonial state, was called Chow.

Both he and his father Wan-wang were men of high and noble character. The prayer offered up at the coronation of his youthful successor, Ching-wan, will give some idea of the principles by which it was considered at the time a good ruler ought to be guided. It was:—"May the king live near to his people and far from flatterers; may he be careful of his time and lavish of his wealth; familiar with the virtuous and the employer of the capable." But these high ideals were far from being generally followed: in the course of time the sovereign of the House of Chow became as degenerate as their predecessors, so that the empire was soon reduced to a state which can only be described as that of chronic anarchy. Its social and political condition, indeed, had created a widespread sense of distrust and insecurity, and it was through this that many able and patriotic men were stirred up to protest, each in his own way, against the degeneracy of the age, and to point out the changes and reforms needed to restore to their country all those advantages which the people had derived in the early days of the empire, from the example and exalted character of their rulers.

It is difficult to form an estimate of the population, or of its distribution, at any fixed period. The very large armies, however, that the feudal princes were able to bring into the field is a proof of its having been considerable. To those who have been in the habit of regarding the Chinese as a thoroughly peaceful race, it must be not a little surprising to find how large a portion of their annals is taken up with battles and the records of military exploits. The main strength of an army consisted, from a very early age, in its chariots, and the manner in which the soldiers were organised and armed is a proof of how very far they had advanced beyond primitive modes of warfare.

A strict ceremonial had been early elaborated, which regulated almost every action and incident of ordinary life; and one is led to ask why it is that mankind so often takes a delight in inventing observances which would seem to serve no other purpose than to reduce existence to a weary round of embarrassing forms. But are they invented? Is it not rather that they are the natural overgrowth produced by age, which often cannot be eradicated without the destruction of the body from which they derive their sustenance. China is hoary with such parasitical growths; since Lâo-tsze's time they have indeed multiplied in every direction with amazing fecundity, and the question naturally arises, whether, under such conditions, it may ever be possible for the Chinese, to rise to the level of those Western nations whose civilisation is the result of influences, which although working at times so silently as to be scarcely observable, are full of youthful vigour and are never at rest?

PART II.

LÂO-TSZE AND HIS PERIOD

LÂO-TSZE AND HIS PERIOD.

SOME seventeen hundred years from the commencement of Chinese history, as made known to us in the pages of the Shoo-King, and in the third year of the reign of the twenty-first sovereign of the dynasty of Chow—answering to the year 604 B.C.—there was born of poor parents in that part of China now known as Honan, a child who was destined to become famous under the designation of Lâo-tsze, the "venerable teacher."

But in his youth he was known only by his family name of Lee, with the honorific addition of Peh-yang, and in his early childhood by that of Urh, apparently from some peculiarity in the form of his ears, as "ear" is the signification of the character in which that sound was expressed.

Of course in after days, the usual supernatural incidents connected with the birth of all great men belonging to his period were related and believed ; but brushing these aside as unworthy of consideration, we have to confess to the very unsatisfactory fact that, apart from a very meagre notice of his life in the " Biographies " of Sze-ma-tsien, the historian, who died about 85 B.C., history tells us very little about him, and gives us no information whatever connected with his childhood, education, or youth.

Sze-ma-tsien has generally been accepted as a reliable authority by his countrymen, and there seems to be little reason for his testimony, so far as it concerns the present subject, being set aside as untrustworthy by those who have nothing better to substitute for it than possibilities and surmises. I have, therefore, in the small amount of data which I have been enabled to put together connected with Lâo-tsze's life, preferred to follow his guidance.

A comparison of dates will show that Lâo-tsze was born fifty-five years before the birth of Confucius and thirty-five before Pythagoras, whilst he preceded Heraclitus, Plato, Protagoras, Anaxagoras, and Socrates by nearly two centuries. He was contemporary with the seven sages of Greece, but Rome was in its infancy. In Babylonia, Nebuchadnezzar, then in the height of his prosperity, was subjugating Judea, destroying Jerusalem, and annihilating the Egyptian power in Asia. Nineveh was razed to the ground the year before Lâo-tsze was born, and three years later Daniel was ennobled for his interpretation of dreams; Ezekiel was giving allegorical illustrations of his prophetic visions; and in Egypt Necho had just failed in his attempt to bring together the waters of the Mediterranean and the Red Sea, whilst Sakya Muni was laying the foundations of a religion which was to be professed by myriads, though the purity of his doctrines was, in the course of time, to be so encrusted and overgrown with puerile superstitions, that the teaching of the great Indian religious reformer is scarcely to be recognised.

That the young Lee Peh-yang must have been endowed with more than ordinary intelligence, combined with all the advantages which belong to a good education, is clearly shown by the fact of his having received the appointment of a Register or Historiographer at the Imperial Court of Chow, then established in the city of Lŏ-yang, to which it had been removed some one hundred and fifty years before. The site of Lŏ-yang was not far from the present provincial town of Ho-nan-foo. It was pleasantly situated in a rich and fruitful valley lying to the south of the Yellow River, between it and a small affluent which runs for some distance parallel to it. A range of low hills sheltered it on the north and separated it from the great river, which is here scarcely more than from half a mile to a mile broad, the current dividing further down, when the water is low, into several shallow channels

separated from each other by flat sandbanks. The
water is very muddy, and the rate at which the
stream flows varies greatly; but in March the current
generally runs at the rate of from two to three miles
an hour. The north shore is flat and indistinct,
whilst the southern banks are very steep. And this
is particularly the case higher up, where the stream
cuts a channel through the loess, so that both banks
are sufficiently high to admit of excavations being
made in them, which have served countless generations as a substitute for houses.

This part of China is not only very fruitful, but
possesses the great charm of exceptional natural
beauty. It has been described as a perfect garden,
whilst the landscape is frequently rendered park-like
by plantations of trees and shrubs, amongst which
the graceful foliage of the waving bamboo stands out
in bold relief against dark groves of cypress.

It was in this city of Lŏ-yang that Lâo-tsze
laboured the greater part of his life, and it was in
its neighbourhood, in his extreme old age, that he
was visited by Confucius.

The duties he had to perform at the Imperial court
were regarded as of the very highest importance, and
belonged to an office which dated from the earliest
historical period. Under the two first dynasties the
number of officials employed as " Historiographers "

was limited to "the Historiographer of the Right" and "the Historiographer of the Left,"—the duty of the former being to register the Imperial edicts and commands, and to take note of such matters as might more especially appertain to the Emperor and his ministers, whilst that of the latter was to record all occurrences and events which might bear upon or illustrate the instruction and general condition of the people.

During the dynasty of Chow (1105 to 242 B.C.) the number of these officials * is said to have been increased to seven, their duties being distributed in the following manner:—The *first* had to take cognizance of, and record, all that concerned the general government of the Empire; the *second*, everything which might be connected with the feudatory states; the *third*, all observations and calculations connected with astronomy; the *fourth*, the noting down of all calamities, unusual events, and phenomena; the *fifth*, the registration of all edicts, ordinances, and legal enactments; the *sixth*, to chronicle all the incidents connected with the royal progresses and expeditions, and to tabulate all information concerning foreigners, including notices of, and translations from, their books; the *seventh* had entrusted to him the preparation of

* See Memoires des Chinois, Paris, 1776, "Sur l'Antiquité des Chinois," p. 70.

memorial notices of the Emperor and members of the
Imperial family.

In addition to these, an official who might be described as the " Register and Keeper of the Archives,"
had somewhat similar—though naturally less important—duties to perform at the court of each of the
feudatory princes.

To which particular department Lee-peh-Yang, or
Lâo-tsze, as we shall hereafter call him, belonged, we
have no knowledge.   Possibly at the commencement
of his career he may have been attached to more than
one, but in any case it can be easily imagined that he
must have had especial facilities for acquiring all that
could be learnt from the state records of the Past;
and it is doubtless to his position as a government
official that he owed his enlarged powers of under-
standing and breadth of thought.   That he had not
wasted his opportunities is made evident from the
frequent quotations from the old writers introduced
by him in his one book.

But what an enormous amount of application the
study of the ancient records and literature must have
required, when it is considered that the form and value
of the characters to be deciphered had undergone
great changes, and that they were either punctured
or engraved on leaves, strips of bamboo, or bits of
wood, previous to the time in which they were written

with some coloured medium on pieces of silk or linen—for paper was as yet unknown. Certainly the arrangement and preservation of a library composed of such materials could have been no light matter.

It was the aggressions of the western Tartars which had occasioned the removal of the capital to Lŏ-yang.

Four centuries earlier the Emperor Mŭh-wang (991 to 936 B.C.) was said to have visited this people, when, under the pretext of a hunting expedition, he had absented himself from his dominions for a considerable period, and the incident has given rise to much speculation as to the distance he may have travelled over, and the nations with whom he may have come into contact. That the records of his progress were existing in Lâo-tsze's time is scarcely to be doubted, though all traces of them disappeared after the destruction of the books ; for the copy of them said to have been discovered in a tomb during the following dynasty is generally acknowledged to be apocryphal. But the little which is known about the matter tends to prove that there was always a certain amount of intercourse between the Chinese and the outside world ; so that it is difficult to believe that they were wholly and entirely ignorant of all that was going on in Western Asia, or that they had never heard of the Assyrians and Babylonians, or of the marvellous cities which formed the centres of their power.

In the case of Lâo-tsze, it is at all events scarcely to be doubted, that many of his ideas were inspired by the writings to which he had access, for it is impossible to regard such thoughts as his as original or spontaneous. All great thoughts may indeed be looked upon as but the sequence and development of antecedent thoughts, less matured perhaps but equally derived, which have passed through the minds of others; and often when we puzzle ourselves by seeking to establish a connection between ideas which seem to flow in the same channels, we should find an easier solution of our difficulties, could we but work backwards until we reached the point of their common origin.

The very education which a man receives, is after all, little more than the assimilation, in a greater or lesser degree, in proportion to individual aptitude, of the slowly aggregated experiences of his predecessors, conveyed in a variety of concrete forms, which are as endless in their combinations as the ceaseless changes of the kaleidoscope; and with the advantages which Lâo-tsze possessed in his own country, I cannot see why it should have been necessary for him to have travelled in the far west —as some declare he must have done—in order to gain such a knowledge of a great over-ruling First Cause, as he sought to promulgate in the pages of the Tâo-tĭh-King.

In the absence, therefore, of any reliable evidence
to the contrary, it is hardly possible to arrive at any
other conclusion than that the greater portion of his
life was spent in study and in the performance of the
duties of his office at Lŏ-yang ; for although he was
living in retirement in the neighbourhood of that
place when visited by Confucius—517 B.C.—he had
then reached extreme old age, and we are told that
he had worked on, until the weakness of his sovereign
and the corruption of the Court, rendered it impossible for him to continue in a position which brought
him in direct contact with so much that was ab-
horrent to his feelings. In this interview with
Confucius he expressed himself very strongly upon
this point, and severely rebuked the Sage for allowing himself to take part in public affairs at a time,
when there was a total absence of either social or
political morality.

It was when he had exhausted this theme, that he
entered upon the subject upon which his thoughts
were chiefly concentrated, the nature and attributes
of the great First Cause, and the relation in which
man stood with respect to Him. Confucius seems to
have borne his upbraidings with all due meekness,
but when the venerable teacher spread out before
him his views on the great mysteries connected with
God, and the creation and government of the world,

he was so completely overcome by the nature of the
revelation conveyed by the old man's words, that he
was reduced to silence, and, it is said, remained for
three days without speaking.   And yet Confucius
could not have been previously ignorant of much
that Lâo-tsze taught, for there is no want of evidence
to show, that from a very early period there had
been a knowledge, however shadowy, of God under
the appellation of "the Taô;" though the meaning
of the word had been altered until it became little
more than an expression for the path, road, or
medium by which the communication was maintained between God and man, though, as often
happens in such cases, "Heaven" and the "Way"
to or from it were often used as if they were synony-
mous terms, and it was in this sense that it was
commonly employed by Confucius.

The question as to whether Tâoism was older than
Lâo-tsze is fully discussed by Dr Legge in his introduction to the Texts of Tâoism—an exhaustive work
which forms the thirty-ninth and fortieth volumes of
the Sacred Books of the East, and to this I refer the
reader who would gain a thorough knowledge of the
subject; but I cannot deny myself the satisfaction of
quoting a passage which lends the great authority of
the learned Professor to the views I have put forward
respecting the antiquity of the belief in the Taon.

Dr Legge says :—" Prolonged study and research have brought me to the conclusion that there was a Tâoism earlier than his ; and that before he wrote the Tâo-tih-King, the principles taught in it had been promulgated, and the ordering of human conduct and government flowing from them inculcated."

With such a clear and authoritative statement as this before us, I think it may be accepted, that it was not needed that Lâo-tsze should have either come from, or travelled in the regions of the West, in order to have acquired the doctrines which were subsequently associated with his name.

At the time of his interview with Confucius, Lâo-tsze must have been approaching his ninetieth year, so that he had reached a very advanced age when he decided on leaving the territory of Chow. But on arriving at the frontier of the State, he was prevailed upon, by the officer who held the post of Warden of the Passes, to stay his steps, until such time as he had committed to writing the opinions, which it is quite evident had already gained him a widespread reputation. Such was the origin of the Tâo-tih-King, or according to the terms in which I have translated it, " Thoughts on the nature and manifestation of God." When it was completed, he passed the frontier and renewed his journey, and from that moment—with but one exception—every record of him ends. This exception is an account, in the writings of his great admirer and disciple Chwang-tsze, who lived between the fourth and third centuries, B.C., of all the details connected with a visit to the house of mourning on the occasion of the old Philosopher's death, paid by one of his disciples. This, if true, and I see no reason why it should not be, disposes of the statement that the time and circumstances of his death were unknown, as well as of the theory that Lâo-tsze's disappearance was due to his return to the country from whence he originally came. For it is pretended by many later critics that he was a foreigner, and from the opinions he professed probably a Brahmin; but I have sought in vain for any direct evidence which would uphold these views. One of our Chinese scholars has, too, gone so far as to deny the authenticity of the Tâo-tih-King, but in this he may be said to stand alone, and to be in opposition to all our most reliable authorities.

It should be understood that the fact of Lâo-tsze having passed the frontier of the state of Chow, did not necessitate his removal from the limits of the Empire.

Of the personality of Lâo-tsze we are told next to nothing. He is frequently represented as a

bald-headed, long bearded, old man riding on an
ox, whilst Confucius is often depicted seated in a
waggon to which an ox is harnessed. A knowledge
of his temperament can only be obtained through
the scanty data afforded by his behaviour to
Confucius in their only interview, which would
lead to the conclusion that he was irascible and
impatient, even when all due allowance is made
for the natural irritability belonging to old age.
Like his great contemporary he was actuated by
the highest and purest motives, but although they
both accepted — in somewhat different degrees —
a great overruling First Cause, and were in perfect
agreement as to the original perfection of man,
they differed widely in their modes of action.
Confucius sought to regenerate society by the
action of Rulers, whose conduct was to be modelled
on that of the great exemplars of the Past, who he
considered to have illustrated, in their persons, all
the virtues it was possible for a man to possess ;
whilst he seemed to give a somewhat secondary place
to that " Great Way "—the " Tâo," which in the eyes
of Lâo-tsze was the Alpha and Omega of all
things in Heaven and Earth ; and whilst recognising
the existence of certain divine powers, he evaded
as far as he possibly could all reference to them,
on the plea, put forth with great candour, that he

did not understand them. Yet he was not wanting
in dogmatic constructiveness when dealing with a
Past from which he eliminated all its defects and
vices.

It will be seen that up to a certain point the doctrines of the two Philosophers were in agreement.
But Lâo-tsze's greater imaginative powers would not
allow him to rest satisfied with a limited purview of
the Past ; nor could he find the perfection he
was seeking for, until he had reached the beginning
of the ages when, as he believed, a primitive people
were endued with a knowledge of the Great First
Cause—" the Great Universal Mother." Then it was,
that society was pure and simple, and free from those
defects which became greater with the growth of
time, until they culminated in a general condition
of depravity such as belonged to his own period.

According to his views, society was originally
pure, because the people knew God. The world
had, then, but to know God and all would be
well ; all human effort outside of this knowledge he
looked upon as worthless, for when the seed is sown
it develops in accordance with natural laws, for
which there is no substitute. It must be confessed
that his ideas on this subject are somewhat hazy,
and it is evident that now and again he encounters
difficulties he does not quite know how to get over,

but it is easy to see that he remains stedfast to the principle he has so much at heart and is ever endeavouring to enforce. And this, no matter the many ways in which he may seek to set it forth, resolves itself into the simple precept, "Believe in God and act in accordance with His laws." All else is made subservient to this.

But how sadly he was misrepresented after his death! His disciples at once sought to find an occult meaning in every word he had uttered, and, as it was with Confucius so with him, he became the central point of a creed. To the creed there naturally followed a ritual, with, in the case of the sect of Tâo, an accompanying priesthood, who subsequently not only borrowed much from Buddhism, but placed all preceding superstitions under contribution, and laid claim to being adepts in necromancy and the magic art. A comparison between the ideas put forward by the great philosopher and metaphysician of the fifth century B.C. and the doctrines professed by his degraded followers in the present day, affords a melancholy proof that time and progress do not always move onward together hand in hand, and that even when a writer may strive to give the clearest possible expression to his thoughts, he will often—as was the case with Lâo-tsze—be completely misunderstood.

D

To us many of his opinions must ever remain obscure and devoid of any solid foundation, and when we regard him in the light of a practical reformer rather than in that of a metaphysician, we shall find him utterly wanting ; for although no exception can be taken to his great precept, " Believe in God and act in obedience to His laws," with respect to the nature of those laws he is extremely vague, unless we include in them the principle of *laissez-faire*, as illustrated by the silent processes of nature, upon which he set so great a value.

Whilst never mentioning Confucius by name or making any direct allusion to his doctrines, it is evident that he looked upon his great contemporary as a dangerous innovator, whose inspirations were derived from a polluted source, and the reader of the Tâo-tih-King is made to feel that many of the passages were written for the purpose of refuting fallacies which he believed would retard rather than advance the return of mankind to those primitive conditions which had marked the genesis of man's social organisation.

I commenced by speaking of Lâo-tsze as a Chinese. But apart from racial peculiarities, I would warn the reader against picturing the old Philosopher to himself as a Chinese of the present day, for with all the continuous flow of that great nation from a source lost in the obscurity of ages, change has asserted itself in China as elsewhere, for never yet was there a fashion which could be called eternal. The dress was very different from that of the Tartar-compelled costume now in use, as may be seen on the vases which possess, or simulate, the stamp of antiquity ; the greatest distinction being, perhaps, in the head coverings and the mode of wearing the hair. In his time, too, all classes sat habitually on mats, from which, when seated in the presence of their master, each disciple rose before venturing to address him. But if time brings changes, it is quite certain it does not always bring progress, for the barbarous and cruel custom of crippling the feet of female children was not introduced till nearly twelve centuries later than the period in which Lâo-tsze and Confucius lived and taught. The impulses which produce human action are indeed full of mystery. No suffi-cient explanation has ever yet been given of the causes which led up to the widespread adoption of such a practice amongst a people who had for years been capable of appreciating and professedly follow-ing the precepts of teachers who enforced the most exalted principles ; for where is anything higher to be found than the " Return good for evil " of Lâo-tsze, and the " Do not to others what you would not have done to yourself " of Confucius.

I think it is hardly possible for anyone to read the "Tâo-tih-King" without much of it coming home to him in a way which gives him a sense of having read it before. Perhaps it is that much modern specula-tion is fast crystalising into forms which have little to distinguish them from the ideas promulgated by the venerable historiographer of the Imperial Court of Chow.

Let us therefore pronounce what opinion we may on Lâo-tsze and his writings, but do not let us forget that some of his opinions—those indeed which we find most difficult of comprehension—are not entirely removed from the sphere of modern thought. As a proof of this I would instance an article on criticism in the *Nineteenth Century* for September 1890, in which the writer says:—

"Yes, the contemplative life, the life that has for its aim not *doing* but *being*, and not being merely but *becoming*, that is what the critical spirit may give us. The Gods live thus. . . . We, too, might live like them, and set ourselves to witness with appropriate emotions the varied scenes that man and nature afford. We might make ourselves spiritual by detaching our-selves from action and becoming perfect by the rejection of energy. . . . From the high tower of Thought we can look out at the world."

Surely this approaches very closely to some of the ideas entertained by Lâo-tsze.

PART III.

THE TÂO-TĬH-KING

OR

THOUGHTS ON THE NATURE AND
MANIFESTATIONS OF GOD

THE TÂO-TĬH-KING,

OR

THOUGHTS ON THE NATURE AND
MANIFESTATIONS OF GOD.

PART I.

CHAPTER I.

GOD (the great everlasting infinite First Cause from whom all things in heaven and earth proceed) can neither be defined nor named.

For the God which can be defined or named is but the Creator, the Great Mother of all those things of which our senses have cognisance.

Now he who would gain a knowledge of the nature and attributes of the nameless and undefinable God, must first set himself free from all earthly desires, for unless he can do this, he will be unable to penetrate the material veil which interposes between him and those spiritual conditions into which he would obtain an insight.

Yet the spiritual and the material, though known

to us under different names, are similar in origin, and issue from the same source, and the same obscurity belongs to both, for deep indeed is the darkness which enshrouds the portals through which we have to pass, in order to gain a knowledge of these mysteries.

CHAPTER II.

When we have gained a knowledge of that which constitutes beauty, we shall also have gained a knowledge of that which constitutes its reverse.

When we have gained a knowledge of that which constitutes goodness, we shall also have gained a knowledge of that which constitutes evil; for all things stand in a mutual relation to each other, and so it has been said—

> " Nothing and something
>   Are relative terms,
> Easy and hard
>   Are the same ;
> The long to the short
>   A proportion affirms,
> Which the high to the low
>   Also claim.
> The tones and the notes
>   Are but modifications,
> And before and behind
>   Only changed situations."

Hence it is that the Sage works when apparently doing nothing, and instructs without uttering a word, ever remembering how all things in nature work silently together; coming into being and possessing nothing; fulfilling the purpose for which they were created without relying on the help of others; advancing to maturity and yet unable to remain in a state of completeness; and yet it is because of this very incapacity for continuance that they are able to continue.

CHAPTER III.

When men of high character are not promoted, the people will not strive to follow their example; just as when those things which are difficult to attain are not valued, thieves will not care to steal them.

In like manner, when objects which would be likely to excite evil desires are kept out of sight, men's minds will not be disturbed by them.

Therefore it is that the wise Ruler, acting on these principles, seeks to keep the minds of his subjects free from evil thoughts, whilst at the same time he fills their bellies with wholesome food; and just in proportion as he seeks to strengthen their bodies, so does he endeavour to weaken their vicious inclinations. His unceasing aim is to prevent their gaining a knowledge of depravity and vice, but should some, however, despite all his efforts, succeed in doing so, he takes care that they shall not have opportunities for making use of it, so that in the end, all, without exception, are rendered amenable to good government.

CHAPTER IV.

God is immaterial, and it is out of the immaterial that He has created all things. Though we know Him not in all His fullness, yet how ·deep and profound He seems, as He stands before us as the Great Universal Progenitor, who

" Blunts the sharp points,
  Sets in order the tangles,
  Attempers the light,
  Brings the atoms together."

Oh, how pure and perfect He is, as He stands before us as the Great Everlasting Preserver.

I know not His origin, but He would appear to have existed before the Lord of Heaven was.

CHAPTER V.

Heaven and Earth do not act from motives of benevolence, but all things in nature are dealt with much in the same way as the artificial dogs stuffed with straw, used in the sacrificial rites, are dealt with.

The Sages were not actuated by mere motives of benevolence, hence they dealt with mankind much in the same manner—that is to say, as instruments.

Heaven and Earth may be likened to the black-smith's bellows, which seems to be empty when it is at rest, but when it is set in motion a continuous stream of air issues from it.

But not so with words, for much talking leads to exhaustion; therefore he who is wise knows when to stop.

CHAPTER VI.

It was written of old—

> " The Spirit of the Valley never dies ;
> The mystic Mother, out whose pregnant womb
> All things have issue.   Hence, too, she is called
> The Root of Nature.   Only hold to this,
> And there will need no labour for its use."

CHAPTER VII.

The fact of Heaven and Earth enduring, is a proof of their having an innate capacity for endurance which does not proceed from their own action or initiative.

So it is that the Sage becomes a leader of others, though he keeps himself in the background; preserves his position, though he places himself on one side; and gains all he seeks for, though he has neither private nor personal aims.

CHAPTER VIII.

Transcendent Goodness is like water.

Water is peaceful and extends its beneficent action throughout Nature, not even disdaining those gloomy depths which the vulgar look upon with horror, for water works much as God does.

Now, the term "Goodness" has a variety of applications. It may refer to the quality of the ground upon which a house stands; or to profundity in a thinker; or to sincerity in a speaker; or to well-ordered government; or to a capacity for doing; or to punctuality; but it is only when goodness is used in reference to freedom from contention that it can be considered faultless.

CHAPTER IX.

It is easier to carry an empty vessel than a full one.

The point which is often felt after it has been sharpened will soon become blunt.

The hall which is filled with silver and gold will not long retain its contents.

He who bears wealth and honours arrogantly will work out his own destruction.

When meritorious services have led to fame, it is time to follow the heavenly rule and retire into obscurity.

CHAPTER X.

He who makes the investigation of his spiritual nature his chief object will be able to bring all his studies to a focus, and this concentration of his energies will render him capable of arriving at a condition of sensibility to impressions similar to that which belongs to a young child.

He who is able to wash himself clean from all obscure and gloomy thoughts, will become sound in mind, and—should he be a ruler—if he govern his people on principles founded on love, he will be able to remain in perfect repose and peace as he watches the processes of Nature proceed around him. He will be as the brood hen who carries on her work when in a state of perfect rest; and who, whilst the light of intelligence may overspread the world, is

able, without knowledge, to procreate and nourish ;
to bring forth, and not retain possession ; to increase
and multiply, and not to hold in subjection ; to act,
and not to depend upon others for assistance.

Well indeed may this be called a deep and impenetrable mystery.

CHAPTER XI.

The thirty spokes of a chariot wheel and the nave
to which they are attached, would be useless, but for
the hollow space in which the axle turns.

The vase moulded out of clay, would be useless,
but for the empty space left for its contents.

The door and window frames of a house would be
useless, but for the empty spaces they enclose, which
permit of ingress and egress, and the admission of
light and air.

This teaches us that, however beneficial the
material may be to us, without the *immaterial* it
would be useless.

CHAPTER XII.

The eye is dazzled by a variety of colours,
The ear is deafened by a diversity of sounds,
The taste is vitiated by a mixture of flavours,

The mind is excited by excessive exercise,
And the character is ruined by seeking to be rich.
Hence it is that the wise man prefers to be emotional rather than to be sensuous, and it is through this that his perceptive faculties become cultivated, so that he is able to arrive at just conclusions.

CHAPTER XIII.

There are two sayings which require explanation—
"Promotion and degradation alike give rise to fear," and "Suffering and honour are alike corporeal."

The meaning of the first is, that he who has been promoted lives in fear that he may be degraded, whilst he who has been degraded is haunted by the dread that his degradation may be continued.

With respect to the second saying, it means that the sense of suffering is a consequence of corporeal existence ; without a body there could be no bodily pain, and for the same reason there would be no personality on whom honour could be bestowed.

This is why he who does honour to his own person, or he who bestows the same love upon others as he does upon himself, may be entrusted with the government of an Empire.

CHAPTER XIV.

That which you look at and cannot see, is called
" invisible."

That which you listen to and cannot hear, is called
" inaudible."

That which you seize upon and cannot grasp, is
called " intangible."

These three definitions are difficult of realisation
when taken singly, let us therefore try what can be
done by bringing them together and uniting them in
One.

The three negations now form a single combination, but if we scrutinise it closely, no matter in what
aspect we may regard it, we shall find nothing either
hidden or revealed; and let us be careful not to
define it or give it a name, or it will escape from us
and become even more subtle than it was before.
This is what is meant by " seeking to define the
indefinable," and " to establish a resemblance between
things which have no real existence."

God is indeed a deep mystery. We cannot recognise His presence; if we advance towards Him we
cannot see what is behind Him; if we follow Him
we cannot see what is before Him. Yet, if we would
gain a knowledge of our present lives, we must hold
on to the God of the Past, and the only clue which

will lead us up to Him is a knowledge of the processes which formed the beginning of that Past.

CHAPTER XV.

The virtues of the olden time, as practised by the
Sages, come down to us in such an exiguous, indefinite,
and obscure form that it is very difficult for us to
understand them. I will however do my best to
make them clear.

That which the Sages took a pleasure in doing may
be likened to the wading across a swollen torrent in
mid-winter.

Their caution resembled that which is produced by
a fear of our associates and of those who live in our
neighbourhood.

Their carriage was as the bearing of a guest
towards his host.

Their self-effacement was as the melting away of
an icicle.

In their indignation they were rough as a piece of
unplaned wood.

Their influence was as far-reaching as the flow of a
mountain torrent, and like the torrent it became
turbid through its own movement.

Now who is there capable of cleansing the impuri-
ties of his nature by tranquillity and rest? And who

is there capable of producing a state of perfect repose by the long-continued calm of a peaceful life?

In conclusion : Those who affect to cherish these principles, and yet have no desire to carry them out in their entirety, will become capable of committing vile actions, and so remain to the end of their lives in an unreformed and imperfect condition.

CHAPTER XVI.

He who would reach the goal of perfect peace,
Must be devoid of self, and carnal thoughts,
For all in Nature stand before our eyes,
And we but watch the changes as they pass,
Returning to the state from whence they came—
That is to say, regaining perfect Peace
By working out the everlasting fate
Which each and all is bound to from the first.
He is enlightened who has well learned this;
But he who knows it not will sink in sin.
He who knows of it will be tolerant,
And being tolerant is therefore just ;
But Justice is the function of a King,
And Royalty an attribute of Heaven,
And what is Heaven-like comes most near to God :
He who is God-like has eternal life,
And so his body passes without harm.

CHAPTER XVII.

In the days of the Great Sovereigns, the time-
honoured ones of antiquity, even the lower orders had
a knowledge of God, and acted upon that knowledge.

Their successors confined themselves to expressing
their admiration and love for Him.

Those who followed, only feared Him.

Then came those who were dissatisfied with Him.

Insufficient faith leads to no faith, and so there
came a time when there was such a falling-off, both
in their words and actions, that even the people were
led to say—" We are self-created."

CHAPTER XVIII.

It was when God had been set aside, that virtue
and benevolence, wisdom and prudence were made
to take his place. As a consequence, there arose a
widespread spirit of deception, so that, at a time
when there was no harmony in the social relations,
filial piety and fraternal affection appeared to flourish,
and ministers claimed to be upright when the whole
fabric of the State was thoroughly depraved and
corrupt.

CHAPTER XIX.

If the world could but get rid of its wisdom and its knowledge, the people would be a hundred times better off: If it could but discard and get rid of its virtue and benevolence, the people would at once return to the practice of filial piety and fraternal affection: If it could but get rid of its cleverness and covetousness, there would be no thieves or robbers.

It may be considered that these three conditions have not been set forth with sufficient clearness. I will therefore give a summary of the practical effects they would produce : Honesty and simplicity would be encouraged, selfishness diminished, and covetousness all but done away with.

CHAPTER XX.

There would be nothing very grievous in renouncing study, for it matters very little, after all, whether we use the character "wei" or the character "ah" for yes; and such knowledge cannot be compared with that which enables us to discriminate between good and evil, and to know that there is a sense of fear in the human heart which cannot be got rid of. Alas! the world is overgrown with weeds, and it is almost impossible to keep them within due bounds. The mass of the people thrive and enjoy themselves like cattle in a rich pasture, and are as happy as he who stands on an elevated terrace in spring. But I, alas! am as a solitary ship at anchor on an unknown shore,—like an infant before it has advanced to the immaturity of childhood. I stand alone amidst an innumerable host living as if there were no return to the state from which they came.

Yes! It must be that the mass of mankind have been granted a superfluity of gifts, whilst I, alone, have been neglected and passed by, for my judgement is weak and my mind is full of doubt.

The vulgar are enlightened and quick witted, whilst I, cannot penetrate the darkness which surrounds me.

The vulgar have knowledge and the spirit of enquiry, whilst I, alas! am full of despair and am like the ocean which knows no rest.

The mass of mankind can find a reason for everything, but my thoughts are foolish and of no account.

Why do I thus differ from others and stand alone? It is because I honour and revere God—the great Mother—to whom we owe our being and all that supports life.

CHAPTER XXI.

The Supreme Good as manifested to us, is an emanation from God—the creative principle of God.

In the beginning there was nought but chaos. Oh, how wild! Oh, how obscure it was!

Then out of its midst came forth forms! Oh, how wild! Oh, how obscure it was!

Out of its midst came material objects. Oh! the stillness—Oh! the darkness—Oh! the stillness.

Out of its midst came forth the forms of life,— perfect in subtlety.

Out of its midst came consciousness, so that from then till now the knowledge of all this remains, and we are enabled to see all that has happened in the world pass in review before us.

Should I be asked, how it is that I have this knowledge of the beginning of all things, I give all that I have now written as my answer.

CHAPTER XXII.

" To amend the depraved,
  To straighten the crooked,
  To fill up the hollows,

To renew the worn out,—
Is what few attain to
Though many attempt it."

It is because the Sage unites these powers in his own person that he is rendered capable of becoming a model for the whole world. He casts a bright light around him, because he has no wish to shine ; he stands out prominently from others, because he is filled with humility ; and it is because he is free from self-assertion, that his merit is acknowledged. It is because of his self-abnegation ' that his work endures, and it is because he is noncontentious, that there is no power upon earth capable of opposing him.

How then, may I ask, can the old saying I have quoted be regarded as a mere repetition of empty words ? Verily, it is so comprehensive that it would be difficult to find anything which is not included in it.

CHAPTER XXIII.

Yet a few words which naturally suggest themselves.

What is it—I would ask—which causes the strong breeze to blow itself out in the course of the morning, and the heavy rain to cease before the close of day ?

The answer is, the action of Heaven and Earth.

But Heaven and Earth, powerful as they may be, are incapable of enduring for ever; and if this be the case with them, how much more must it be so with Man.

Remember however that the man who regulates all his actions by a belief in God, will become like unto God; just as he who walks in the path of virtue will become virtuous; and he who pursues a course of vice will become vicious.

But he who has become like unto God will be a servant of God, whilst he who has become virtuous will obey the dictates of virtue, and he who has become vicious will continue to be a slave to vice.

To have a weak faith is to have no Faith.

CHAPTER XXIV.

Just as he who raises himself on his toes is unable to stand firmly, or he who straddles out his legs to walk easily, so will he who sees nothing outside himself be incapable of becoming intelligent. So, too, it is, that he who thinks he is always right, will never emerge from obscurity; nor he who boasts of his own merits, stand high in the opinion of his fellows; nor he who has no pity but for himself, live long in the remembrance of others.

Such modes of proceeding, when compared with the divine principles of action emanating from God, present themselves to us much as the off-scourings of food and other loathsome matters held in universal detestation might do.

‘ Hence it is that the Godly man is careful to eschew all such conduct.

CHAPTER XXV.

Before Heaven and earth were,
Naught but deep silence
Reigned o'er a void
Of endless immensity,—
Dead, for no breath
Of life had yet breathed there :
Oh, how silent, how void it was !
Then He the Infinite,
Perfect, Immutable,
Moved through this nothingness ;
He, the Creator,
The " Mother " of all things.
I, in my ignorance,
Knowing no name for Him,
Speak of Him only
As " God," the Eternal,
Thus in one word

Including His attributes :
He, the All-Knowing,
The All-Pervading,
Ever-existent ;
Near—yet so far off.
Man's laws are earthly,
Nature's are Heaven-born,
Yet one and both come
From God, the great Source
And Centre of all Law.

CHAPTER XXVI.

Gravity is the source of lightness, and rest the controlling power of motion.

Therefore it is that the wise man does not—even when making but a day's journey—separate from his baggage-waggons, so that should a beautiful view spread itself out before him, he rests a while, and then continues his journey.

Hence, too, the Ruler who acts with levity, will lose the subjects who form the very root of his power, whilst should he act with undue haste, he will lose his Kingdom.

CHAPTER XXVII.

A good walker moves lightly over the ground, and his footsteps leave no trace.

A good speaker is accurate and keeps his temper.

A good reckoner needs no tablets.

A good smith needs no wooden bars, yet the doors he fastens cannot be opened.

A skilful joiner needs no cords to keep his work together.

In the same manner, it is through the skill and ability of the Sage, that his fellow-men are aided without one of them being discarded or lost, and it is the same when he deals with the brute creation or material objects.

This is what is called being " doubly enlightened," and hence it is that the skilful man becomes the unskilful man's master, and the unskilful man becomes the skilful man's slave.

When the slave does not honour his master, and the master does not love his slave, although they may both have a knowledge of what is suitable, they will be guilty of gross stupidity.

This may be considered an abstract of the leading principles belonging to a very difficult and subtle subject.

CHAPTER XXVIII.

" He who puts forth his strength
And keeps back his weakness,
Is like a deep river
Into which all the streams flow.

His virtue shall wane not
Until he is, once more,
As pure as in childhood."

" He who shows forth his light
And hides all his darkness,
Shall serve as a model
To all in the Empire.
Hence it is that his virtue
Shall be lasting and fail not
Till merged in the infinite."

" He who makes known his glory
And sets shame behind him,
Shall be like a valley
In which all take refuge.
Abounding in virtue
His gifts shall suffice him
Till restored to his elements."

It is out of the simple elements into which every thing in nature resolves itself that all material objects are formed : and in like manner the Sage, by making use of the constituents he finds at hand, is able to build up a stable government and establish laws, which shall not be unduly severe on a substantial basis.

CHAPTER XXIX.

He who seizes upon an Empire from ambitious motives, will not succeed, for an Empire is a divine institution, and he who thinks he has the power of making it, will mar it ; and he who thinks he has the power of ruling it by mere force of will, will lose it. For truly, as the old saw has it—

> " While some advance
> The rest retire,
> While some inhale
> The rest respire,
> While some are weak
> The rest are strong,
> While some stand still.
> The rest move on."

Therefore the Wise-man endeavours to keep within due bounds, and avoid all exaggeration, luxury, and extravagance.

CHAPTER XXX.

He who would assist a Ruler by the application of principles proceeding from a knowledge of God, is far more likely to succeed, than he who would coerce an Empire by the adoption of stringent military measures, for where large armies are es-tablished, thorns and thistles grow apace, and where they march, pestilence and famine follow in their footsteps.

The wise ruler rests satisfied when he has gained his point, and does not presume, because he has succeeded, to adopt arbitrary measures ; neither does

he allow his achievement to make him either pre-
sumptuous, boastful, or arrogant. Should he, however, be compelled to take further action, he is careful to guard himself from being led, by any subsequent success, to adopt a line of conduct that may
be either harsh or tyrannical.

But all things pass through maturity to old age,
which is as much as to say, they are not God-like, for
all that is not God-like soon comes to an end.

CHAPTER XXXI.

However excellent warlike weapons may be, they
cannot be regarded as auspicious instruments, and
it is because of the universal dislike entertained
towards them, that they have no place in the system
of the Statesman whose action is regulated by divine
principles.

In the dwelling of the Superior Man, the place of
honour is on the left, but that of the soldier, in the
military movements and exercises, is on the right,
for the soldier, like the weapon, is not an instrument
of happy augury. The instruments used by the
Superior Man are very different, and even when
they fail him, he makes use of none other.

The great object of the Superior Man is to preserve peace and tranquillity. He takes no pleasure in winning battles, for he knows that if he did so, he would be finding gratification in the slaughter of his fellows, and he believes that he who takes delight in the destruction of his fellow-men, will never succeed in gaining the affection of those he rules over.

In all that is auspicious the left occupies the highest place ; in all that is inauspicious—the right. So it is that in the army the second in command is placed on the left, whilst the General in Chief is on the right, and this accords with the position which has the place of honour in the funeral Rites.

Truly, he who kills numbers of men, should mourn over them and weep over them, and a victorious battle, should be celebrated with the same rites as are appointed for a funeral.

CHAPTER XXXII.

"God is unchanging and has no name."

Now, although this statement is so short and so simple, the world cannot take it in. Yet if Kings and Princes were but to receive it, there is nothing under Heaven which would not resort to them, and it would produce a spirit of harmony which would descend upon the Empire like a fragrant dew, so that the people would no longer require to receive orders from their superiors, but would be rendered capable of controlling their own actions.

But when a name was given to the Great First Cause, which has been continued to this day, the knowledge I speak of became arrested, and we soon cease to be familiar with that which is withheld from us.

Ah! if the right knowledge of God, were but spread through the Empire, it would become like the Ocean and great rivers into which the rivulets and streams continuously flow.

CHAPTER XXXIII.

He who has a knowledge of other men, is intelligent, but he who has a knowledge of himself, is enlightened.

He who gains a victory over other men, is strong, but he who gains a victory over himself, is all powerful.

He who is temperate is rich, but he who is energetic has strength of purpose.

He who does not waste his vital powers, may live long, but he who dies and is not forgotten, will be immortal.

CHAPTER XXXIV.

How Infinite and all-pervading God is! All nature turns towards Him for support and sustenance, and He withholds nothing. It is impossible to find a name for His perfections. He bestows His love and care on all that He has created, yet demands nothing in return. Passionless and Eternal, His glory is exhibited in the smallest of His works. All nature reverts to Him, and though He seeks not to exalt Himself He is revealed to us by His greatness.

Hence it is that the Sage, during the course of his whole life, never seeks to be great, and this is why he is able to reach the very pinnacle of greatness.

CHAPTER XXXV.

All the people in the Empire will rally round the Ruler, who is able to realise the grand conception which belongs to God.

They will not only rally round him, but they will cease from evil-doing and become calm, peaceful, and contented.

He who entertains a guest with music and feasting, will give him pleasure, and make him unwilling to depart; but should he open his mouth and speak to

F

him of God, ah! how tasteless and unattractive his words would seem.   But although what we see and hear of God is so dim and indistinct, yet His power, to those who seek to use it, is inexhaustible.

CHAPTER XXXVI.

That which is about to contract, must be in a state of expansion.

That which is about to become weak, must be strong.

That which is about to fall down, must stand up.

That which is about to be stolen, must be in its place.

All this is but a vague way of saying :—Austerity is overcome by gentleness, and strength is vanquished by weakness.   Hence it would be as idle to attempt the reformation of a state by severe measures, as it would be to try and catch fish in the depths of an abyss.

CHAPTER XXXVII.

God is eternally at rest, yet there is nothing that he does not do.

If kings and princes would but hold fast to this, all under their rule would work out their own reformation. But if after they had done this it might be found necessary to act, I would control them by adopting, as far as possible, those pure and simple principles which belong to the Great Nameless One.

> The simple nature of the Nameless One
> Will free us from desire, and so give Peace,
> And peaceful states, will govern best themselves.

PART II.

CHAPTER XXXVIII.

Virtue, is not the highest of all the influences which emanate from God, and therefore it is that it exists.

It is not because of their having fallen away from virtue, that the minor influences are secondary, but because they are without it.

The higher influences are passive, and aimless.

The lower influences are active, and work with a motive.

Transcendent benevolence is active, and works without a motive.

Transcendent integrity is active, and works with a motive.

Transcendent propriety is active, but when it is not exercised it has to be enforced.

Hence it came to pass that, when the knowledge of God was lost, it was replaced by virtue; that when the knowledge of virtue was lost, it was replaced by benevolence; that when the knowledge of benevolence was lost, it was replaced by integrity; and that when the knowledge of integrity was lost, it was replaced by propriety. But propriety in itself is little more than the counterfeit of sincerity and truth, and becomes in consequence the frequent cause of confusion and disorder.

From this it will be seen, that when we study the past it presents itself to us under two distinct aspects —that of a flower from God's own hand, and that of the commencement of human folly, and so it is that the Superior man seeks to establish himself on a firm and substantial basis, and to avoid all that is weak and frivolous. He endeavours to gather the fruit and not the flower, and is consequently enabled to discriminate between the good and the evil, the complete and the immature.

CHAPTER XXXIX.

In the early days of the world, God was in close union with—

The heavens, through their purity,
The earth, through its repose,

The gods, through their spirituality,

The vallies, through their fruitfulness,

Living creatures, through their fecundity,

Kings and Princes, that the world might be well
governed.

These were the causes which led to this union, for
—Without purity, the heavens would have been in
danger of being rent ; without repose, the earth would
have been in danger of becoming unstable ; without
spirituality, the Gods would have been in danger of
becoming extinct ; without fruitfulness, the vallies
would have been in danger of becoming deserts ;
without fecundity, living things would have been in
danger of dying out ; and without humility, Kings
and Princes would have been incapable of good
government, and would have been in danger of being
overthrown.

From this last we learn, that to honour the needy
and to exalt the lowly, is the very root and foundation of all power, and it is for this reason that Kings
and Princes, when speaking of themselves, use de-
preciatory terms, such as " the fatherless one," or " the
lone one," or " the solitary one," and does not this of
itself show us, that they regarded humility as the
true foundation upon which all action should be
based. They knew that to lay down many
foundations, is to have no foundation, and so it was

that they had no wish to have either the dazzling splendour of a precious gem, or the hardness and incompressibility of a piece of stone.

CHAPTER XL.

Retrogression, is one of God's methods ;
Weakness, is one of God's agents.

All things in nature are born material, but the material is evolved from the immaterial.

CHAPTER XLI.

When scholars of the highest grade, hear of the doctrines based upon a belief in God, they do their best to learn and practise them.

When scholars of average ability, hear of them, they seek to preserve them for a time, whilst at other times they give them no heed.

When the lowest class of scholars, hear of them, they are turned into ridicule by the majority of them, whilst to the remainder they are incomprehensible. Hence of these it has been said—

> " Their greatest brightness is but a dark shade,
> Their feeble movements ever retrograde ;
> They seek to rise, and grovel on the ground ;
> Their highest virtue, in low depths is found ;

They would be pure, whilst wallowing in shame ;
They dare bestow, that which they cannot claim ;
Virtue the base, on which they fain would stand ;
Whilst rapine reigns, supreme throughout the land."

As a vast enclosure, the boundaries of which cannot be seen ; as a great unfinished vessel, moving onwards towards completion ; as a mighty voice, the tones of which are rarely heard ; as a great figure, without form and void ; so God presents Himself to us in all His namelessness and obscurity. But it is by God alone, that all goodness is bestowed and perfected.

CHAPTER XLII.

One, was created by God. From One, came Two ; Two, produced Three ; and from Three, all things proceeded in a continuous succession, emerging from darkness into light, and brought into harmony by the divine afflatus.

As I have already said, Kings and Princes, when speaking of themselves, do so in terms of disparagement, such as " the fatherless one " or " the solitary one," or "the worthless one," for : " He who humbleth himself shall be exalted," and " He who exalteth himself shall be humbled."

This is a principle which other men have taught, and it is what I also teach. No opposition or obstruction can destroy it, and this is why I have made it the groundwork of my teaching.

CHAPTER XLIII.

The most yielding element in nature—water—can dash against, and wear away, the most solid substances; and it does not require a crevice, to enable the immaterial to penetrate the material.

It was a knowledge of this, which first led me to recognise the advantage of what may be called the action of inaction, and the instruction to be conveyed by silence. But there are very few people in the world, who are capable of accepting the usefulness of inaction.

CHAPTER XLIV.

Which is the best—the love of self, or Fame?
A life of pleasure, or an honoured name?
Which is the evil most to be deplored,
The loss of riches or a plenteous hoard?
Know this—that he, who gives way to desire,
Will burn his life out, in fierce passions' fire;
And he whose mind is set on gems and gold
Will find them easier far to gain, than hold.
But with contentment, there is no disgrace,
And moderation, gives a long-lived race.

CHAPTER XLV.

The wise man regards his greatest gifts as mere broken vessels, which, though imperfect, are still capable of being used.

However complete his knowledge, he looks upon himself as so ignorant, that he lives in fear of being reduced to extremities.

No matter how upright he may be, he is only conscious of his own depravity.

The honour he receives from others, has no other effect than that of making him feel like a hypocrite.

And however eloquent he may be, he is painfully impressed with the feeling that he is slow of speech.

Just as rapid exercise will warm us when we are cold ; so will perfect stillness cool us when we are hot.

Purity and peace, form the standard according to which the whole world is regulated.

CHAPTER XLVI.

Were the Empire to be governed in accordance with the divine principles emanating from God, swift horses would only be used for work in the fields ; but if it be not governed on those principles, war horses will be bred on the frontiers.

There is no greater crime than inordinate desire; no greater misfortune than discontent; nor anything more blameable than covetousness. Hence the saying that—

" He who is contented will always have enough."

CHAPTER XLVII.

Without going outside my own door, I can gain a knowledge of the world ; and without looking out of my own window, I can see the roads which lead up to heaven, though the farther they recede from me, the smaller they appear, and the less I know about them.

This it is which enables the Sage to reach the goal without exertion, to find a name for that which he does not see, and to bring his task to completion when he is, apparently, doing nothing.

CHAPTER XLVIII.

Study, will produce a daily increase of knowledge, but a seeking after God, will lead to a daily diminution of the passions, and this diminution will steadily continue till they cease to exist. Then it is that he who has reached this point will find there is nothing he is not capable of doing.

He who knows how to let things alone may become the Master of an Empire; but he who is always endeavouring to do something will fail through want of strength.

CHAPTER XLIX.

The Superior Man has no rigid rules of conduct, but acts in conformity with the views of those over whom he is placed.

In my case, I act with equal kindness to all whether good or evil, and thus all become good.

In like manner I equally accept truth and falsehood, and hence all become truthful.

The Superior Man is in constant fear lest his intercourse with the world should make him worldly: The eyes of all the people are turned towards him, and he in his turn looks upon them as his children.

CHAPTER L.

We issue into life, only that we may enter into death.

Should thirteen represent the number of those who come forth into life, then thirteen will represent the number of those who go forth into death, and thirteen of those who were born into the world will have moved steadily onward, from the cradle to the grave.

Why does life thus end in death? It is, that life can only be sustained by the expenditure of vitality.

Now, it was said of old that he who knew how to maintain his vital powers, would be able to pass without danger through a path infested by the rhinoceros and tiger; and that he might go into battle without having provided himself with either armour or weapons, for the rhinoceros would not be able to find a vulnerable spot in which to thrust his horn, or the tiger a place into which he could dig his claws, or the soldier a weak point into which he could drive his sword!

And why was this?

Simply because he who was thus invulnerable, had become so, through having destroyed the power of death.

CHAPTER LI.

God gives us life; and life is supported by the gifts which emanate from Him. We are formed out of the materials created by His hand, and perfected by his power.

Therefore it is that all in the world bow down

before God and reverently meditate upon His nature and attributes.

But the honour and reverence paid to God, is no mere act of obedience to some command or decree, but a spontaneous feeling which has existed through all eternity.

For God creates and nourishes. He gives us offspring and length of days, and it is through Him that all things are sustained and protected, and arrive at maturity and completeness.

God creates, and does not retain ; He acts, and has no selfish motive ; He gives a continuous increase, and does not assert His supremacy ; how truly mysterious and inscrutable must, then, His nature ever be to us.

CHAPTER LII.

In the beginning all things proceeded from God— 丿丁丁 the Universal Mother—and we gain a knowledge of Him through His works, just as we gain an insight into the character of a mother, by studying that of her children. Let a man but preserve and act upon this knowledge of God, and then, although his body may pass away, he will receive no harm.

He who is reticent, and guards himself against outward impressions, will reach the end of life without effort, but he who is careless in these particulars, will find that his whole life has been thrown away.

Intelligence, is formed by minute observation, and strength, by the conservation of the germs of vital energy.

He who uses aright the light which has been bestowed upon him, will enter into that state of intelligence which is one of the chief attributes of God, and his body shall be set free from all calamity and suffering :—this is what is meant by " being clothed with immortality."

CHAPTER LIII.

If, perchance, I should have sufficient knowledge to permit of my walking in the Right Way, my great fear would be as to my being able to induce others to follow my example, for though the Great Way is very easy, the people love to follow the by-paths. Hence it is that whilst the palaces have many steps, the fields are overgrown with weeds, and the granaries hold no corn ; and that, too, whilst the Princes wear gorgeous robes and sharp swords, gorge themselves with food and drink, and have a superfluity of wealth. This indeed may be called the glorification of plunder, but it is very far from the practice of the principles emanating from God.

CHAPTER LIV.

Those who build on a sure foundation—that is to say, on the principles emanating from God—shall be firmly established ; and for those who cling to them, there shall be no falling away.

Their progeny shall be continued through successive generations, and the sacrificial rights shall never fail them.

They who cultivate these principles in their own persons will become sincere ; extending them to their families, they will flourish ; spreading them abroad amongst the villagers, they will multiply ; making them the rule of government, the State will become powerful ; and sowing them broadcast over the Empire, they will spring up on every side and produce a plentiful harvest of happiness and prosperity.

Thus it is that—

> " He who would know
> His fellow-men,
> Must learn to know
> Himself, and then
> In his own home
> He e'er will find

All that he needs
  To know, mankind.
He need not rove
  His native State,
The outer world
  Will illustrate,
And it is in
  The Flowery land
He best will see
  How empires stand."

If I should be asked how I know this; all that I have now written would be my answer.

CHAPTER LV.

He who is largely endowed with the virtue which emanates from God, may be liked unto a newly-born babe, which fears neither the claws of a wild beast, nor the stings of venomous insects, nor the swoop of a bird of prey ; and which, although the bones and muscles are still weak, has a firm grasp; whilst its state of perfect innocence is combined with evidences of those future conditions which belong to its virile nature. It may cry all day long without its voice being injured, because those very cries form a part of that harmony which governs its existence.

Who knows of this
  Is the Unchanging One :
Who knows of Him
  Sees clearly all the rest.

If life have length,
    It is no cause for joy,
For with each breath—
    Tho' it may give us strength—
We ripen daily,
    Moving on to death.

And this is why it is said we do not resemble God, for there is nothing in the nature of God which is transient.

CHAPTER LVI.

He who knows God, does not talk about Him.

He who is always talking about God, does not know Him.

He who knows God sets a watch over himself, and acts in such a way as to bring himself into a mysterious conformity with Him.

Hence he becomes invulnerable to either familiar- | ity or coldness; to benefits or injuries; to honour or contempt; and thus it is that the whole world pays him homage.

CHAPTER LVII.

It is by justice, that a Kingdom is governed; by stratagems, that soldiers are best made use of; and by non-interference, that an Empire is gained over. If you ask me how I know this, I answer :—

G

If in an Empire the people are hampered by restrictions and regulations, they will gradually become poorer and poorer; if they are only made the means for producing wealth, there will be endless confusion; if they are made unduly intelligent and skilful, society will become too artificial and luxurious; and if the laws are too clearly defined, so that they can be easily evaded, there will be an increased number of thieves and robbers.

Hence it was the Sage said :—" I will let the people alone, and they will reform themselves; by loving peace and justice myself, I shall teach the people to follow my example; through my non-interference they will become rich, and from having no ambitions of my own, I shall be able to teach them the advantages which belong to a simple and contented life."

CHAPTER LVIII.

" The rule which to the world most grievous seems,
  Is oft the one that with most blessings teems ;
  That rule which is in all things most exact,
  Not seldom fails through being void of tact."

How is it that misery so often proceeds from happiness, and that happiness is so often found concealed in the lap of misery? Alas! alas! who can tell what may be the end of either?

To the unjust, justice appears in a strange garb,

and goodness, as the monstrous creation of a popular delusion which takes a long time to die out. Hence the Sage—

> Would set all square and free from harm,
> Be moderate and seek to calm,
> Takes a firm stand nor wastes his might,
> And shines, but with a softened light.

CHAPTER LIX.

In the management of men, and in the service of Heaven, there is no quality of greater value than moderation.

But this moderation is only one of a rich endowment of virtues, which may be obtained by careful training in youth ; there are no difficulties which may not be overcome by a man who has been so prepared, and it is impossible to say what he may not attain to. He may even become the Ruler of his state, and should he at the same time be possessed by the Spirit of God, his reign will be a long one, for the principle of longevity is shown by the experience of all ages to be that—the root which strikes down deepest will last longest.

CHAPTER LX.

There is, comparatively, as much care required in cooking a small fish, as there is in the government of a large State.

When the Empire is ruled in accordance with divine principles, the malign influences are reduced to inaction; it is not that they have lost their power, but that they are rendered incapable of using it in a way that may be injurious to mankind.

They still possess the power of injuring mankind, but since it is neither exercised by them nor by the just Ruler, this mutual forbearance necessarily leads to the establishment, and general acceptance, of those perfect principles which emanate from God.

CHAPTER LXI.

A large State should be like a river running through a plain, into which all the smaller streams discharge themselves.

It should, in fact, imitate the conditions which have been imposed by nature on the weaker sex; for it is by quiescence that the female attracts and receives the homage of the male. Thus it is that if a large State humbles itself before the smaller States, it will gain their fealty, and if the small States humble themselves before a large one, they will gain its protection. The end being attained in both cases by the same means.

The object sought for by the large State would be aggrandisement, that of the smaller one protection, and both would have obtained that of which it had the greatest need.

From this we plainly see that for the great, equally with the small, humility has its advantages.

CHAPTER LXII.

God, is the universal refuge, the good man's treasure, and the bad man's sustainer.

Now, eloquence may be profitable to the man who possesses it; and honourable conduct may conduce to prosperity; but by what means is it possible to get rid of the effects of a man's vileness?

The Emperor may be seated on the throne, and the power of the great feudatory States may be established, yet neither he who grasps the sceptre with both hands, nor he who takes precedence in a chariot drawn by four horses, is equal to him who, without moving from his seat, advances steadily God-wards.

How, let me ask, did the ancients seek to do honour to God?

Was it not by beseeching Him daily to pardon their offences? Yes, truly! and that was the cause of his being held in such universal veneration.

CHAPTER LXIII.

When God is held in high honour throughout the Empire, then its Ruler will do most, when appearing to do least; work hardest, when apparently taking his ease; enjoy all things, without seeming to make use of his senses; turn the small into the great, and the few into the many; and *requite evil with good.* He will make that which is difficult, easy, break up the whole into its component parts, and dealing with all the intricate questions connected with the government of the Empire, in the same spirit, he will find that they have been made comparatively simple.

Hence it is that a Wise Ruler, though he may not seek to do great things, will be able to achieve them by a minute attention to details.

Just as promises which are lightly made are lightly broken, so are things which appear most easy to accomplish often those which lead us most easily into difficulties.

Therefore he who is wise looks at all things in the light of their difficulties, and by so doing, he is sure, in the end, to find that they can be overcome.

CHAPTER LXIV.

That which is at rest, is easily maintained in its position.

That which has not been foreseen, is easily deliberated upon.

* There is no emphasis on this sentence in the original.

That which is brittle, is easily broken.

That which is minutely divided, is easily scattered.

It is easier to prevent, than to suppress; to establish a good government, than to restore it.

Remember that the tree which you can barely clasp with both arms, has grown up from a filament almost as fine as a hair; that a tower of nine stories, rests upon a small mound of earth; and that a journey of a thousand li, commences with a single step.

He who is in a state of unrest, will defeat his own purpose, just as he who never relaxes his grasp, will in the end lose his hold.

This is why the Sage prefers a state of inactivity, for then he is neither unsuccessful or defeated.

When people take an active part in anything, they are often unsuccessful through failing to remember, that the conclusion of an affair, requires as much careful consideration as it did at its commencement.

Hence the great aim of the Sage is to have no desires; to set no value on objects difficult to obtain; to learn and not merely to study; and to avoid the very popular error of endeavouring to assist the processes of nature, which is what he never ventures upon doing.

CHAPTER XLV.

Those in the olden time, who acted in accordance with the principles emanating from God, did not employ them as a means for enlightening the people, but as a means for restoring them to a state of guilelessness and simplicity.

The greatest difficulty in governing proceeds from the people knowing too much. Therefore it is, that he who seeks to govern a Kingdom by increasing the knowledge of the people, is an enemy to his country, whilst he who seeks to govern a Kingdom without endeavouring to make everybody wise, is its benefactor.

A knowledge of these two methods will give us a standard for the regulation of our actions; but the eternal knowledge of which these regulating principles are the outcome, belongs to the mysteries of the Divine nature, which we are unable to penetrate; yet how deep and far-reaching they are, and how antagonistic to material ideas! It is through them alone that we arrive at harmony.

CHAPTER LXVI.

Why do the Oceans and great rivers exercise a supremacy over the water channels and streams?

It is because the Oceans and great rivers stand at a lower level, and hence the rivulets and streams, are compelled to become their tributaries.

In like manner the Sage, when he wishes to dominate over a people, is careful to speak humbly to them. When he wishes to lead, he keeps himself in the background, and by so doing he gains his end without having created a feeling amongst the people, that they have been either injured or oppressed ; thus the spirit of disobedience has no place, and the Empire is filled with joy. He himself avoiding all strife, how is it possible for others to contend with him ?

CHAPTER LXVII.

In the Empire all call me great ; but if this be true, degeneracy must be greatness, and degeneracy and improvement must have the same meaning. A puzzling idea which it would take a long time to analyse.

Now I possess three treasures which I hold fast to and cherish.

The first is love (such as felt by parents for their children, by a householder for his home, or by a patriot for his country) ; the second is thrift ; and the third is humility, such as keeps me from striving for the first place in the Empire.

It is this love which gives me courage ; it is through this thrift that I am enabled to be liberal ; and it is because I dare not aspire to become the first man in the Empire, that it is rendered possible for me to develop my character to its highest point.

In the present day men seek to be courageous without love; to be liberal without thrift; and to occupy high places without humility. This is not life, but death!

It is this love, which gives its possessor the victory in battle, and enables him to preserve that over which he keeps guard.

For Heaven bestows the power of loving on those it would succour and protect.

CHAPTER LXVIII.

The best leader, is not he who is most pugnacious.

The best fighter, is he who can control his temper.

The greatest victories, are those gained without strife.

He who knows how to make himself subservient to others, will be best able to make the best use of them.

This is what is meant when men speak of "acting in a peaceful spirit"; of "making the best use of men's energies"; and of "seeking to work in harmony with Heaven." Which last, the ancients regarded as the highest aim of all human effort.

CHAPTER LXIX.

It was once said by a military leader, "When I find I cannot act the host"—that is attack—"I play the guest "—that is, act on the defensive—" and when I find I cannot advance an inch, I retire an ell."

So it is that we speak of " making progress " when we do not advance ; of " holding our own " when we have no hands to grasp with ; of " out-manœuvring the enemy " when there is no one to oppose ; and of " defending our position " when we have no weapons.

It is a great misfortune to hold an enemy in contempt, for it may lead to the loss of all that we most value ; and hence it is that when soldiers engage in close combat, the victory will belong to him who is actuated by the highest motive—that is, love for his family and country.

CHAPTER LXX.

Although my words are extremely simple and easy to put into practice, yet, throughout the empire they are neither understood nor acted upon.

Now all words proceed from some original source, and all affairs are regulated by some controlling power, and it is those who are ignorant of this who ignore me.

Those who comprehend me are indeed few, but so it is, I have the more honour.

It was because of this that the holy ones of old clad themselves in hair-cloth, and hid their most precious gifts in their bosoms.

CHAPTER LXXI.

A knowledge of our own ignorance, is a proof of superiority, but ignorance of our own knowledge, is nothing less than a mental malady, which, like all other maladies, will be best escaped by those who have a dread of the sufferings it will give rise to.

It was because the holy ones of old dreaded its effects, that they never suffered from this malady.

CHAPTER LXXII.

Some great calamity will befall those who have no abiding fear of that which ought to inspire awe.

Do not despise the place in which you dwell, or be dissatisfied with your lot in life, for happiness belongs only to the contented.

Hence the Sage studies himself, and does not become selfish; and cultivates self-respect without becoming vain. It is this which renders him capable of discriminating between right and wrong.

CHAPTER LXXIII.

He whose courage amounts to rashness, will lose his life, but he in whom it is tempered with discretion, will save it.

The one quality is prejudicial to its possessor, the other is beneficial.

Who can tell why it is that Heaven holds anything in abhorrence? Even to the Sages this is a question which presents the greatest difficulties.

These are the principles upon which Heaven is said to act :—

> " Without a fight
>   To gain the day,
> Without a word
>   To enforce its sway,
> Without a call
>   To draw all near,
> Without a plan
>   To make things clear.
> Heaven's net is vast,
>   Its meshes gape,
> And yet, alas !
>   None can escape."

CHAPTER LXXIV.

If the people do not fear death, how can they be restrained from crime by the dread of capital punishment ?

But if the people are brought up in fear of it, then, should a criminal be seized at once and executed, none would dare to follow his example.

It is usual for the sentence of death to be carried out by an officer appointed for that purpose. To act otherwise is much as if a man set to work to chop up wood instead of employing a woodcutter. The chances are that if he did so he would cut his own fingers.

CHAPTER LXXV.

When a Prince impoverishes his country by the multiplication of taxes, the people will starve, and there is nothing makes the government of a State more difficult, than when the people know that the cause of their suffering is to be found in the action of their Rulers.

When the whole energies of a people are expended on endeavouring to support life, they will make light of death. But he who takes no heed of life, is wiser than he who sets an undue value on it.

CHAPTER LXXVI.

Man, when first born, is weak and flexible, but in death he becomes rigid and unbending.

Trees and plants, when they begin to grow, are soft and easily broken, but when they die, they become dry and rotten.

Therefore, hardness and rigidity, belong to death, whilst softness and pliability belong to life.

Hence it is that the army which is wanting in flexibility, will be defeated, and the tree which has arrived at the solidity of maturity, will be cut down.

From this we see that tenderness and flexibility, stand on higher ground than rigidity and strength.

CHAPTER LXXVII.

Heaven acts in much the same way as the archer does. The archer, when about to use his bow, raises the end which was undermost, and lowers the end which was uppermost; and corrects his aim by reducing the elevation should it be too great, or by increasing it should it be too small. In like manner, heaven diminishes the superfluous, and adds to that which is incomplete.

But man's mode of action is very different, for he takes from those who are in need in order to increase the superfluities of the rich; and it is he, alone, who is influenced by a knowledge of God, who is rendered capable of applying that which he doth not lack to the wants of others.

Hence the Superior man does not rely on his own action, or stand upon his own merits, or blazon forth his own goodness.

CHAPTER LXXVIII.

Of all that there is soft and yielding in nature, there is nothing softer or more yielding than water; yet for the reduction of hard substances there is nothing can surpass it.

This proves that the strong can be mastered by the weak, and the hard and inflexible by the soft and yielding.

Yet though this is universally known, how rare it is to find anyone capable of giving it a practical application.

Hence it was once said by a Sage :—

"The fields are spread over with filth, and the fructifying power it produces is spoken of as 'the Spirit of the harvest.'

"The land is full of misery, and the regulating force it necessitates is called 'the Sovereignty of the State.'"

These are apparent contradictions, but they are none the less true.

CHAPTER LXXIX.

When a great quarrel has been made up, a certain degree of soreness will remain, and the question is, how this soreness can best be put an end to.

It was a consideration of this kind, which made the Sage retain the left hand corner of a bond, after he had relinquished his claim upon it; for though to the virtuous man, a bond is sacred, the vicious man, often uses it as an instrument of extortion.

Though Heaven is ever impartial, it is always found on the side of the good.

CHAPTER LXXX.

Were I the ruler over a small and sparsely-peopled country, though I should provide arms for some tens or hundreds of my subjects, I would take care that they were not required to be used.

I should bring up my people in the fear of death, and endeavour to deprive them of any wish to emigrate; and though they might possess boats and carriages, I would not allow them to be used for travelling; neither would I permit them to make any public display of their armour or weapons.

I would try and make my people return to a state of primitive simplicity, like that of the time in which knotted cords were used instead of writing, so that

H

their food would seem sweeter, their clothing better, their houses more comfortable, and their lives brighter to them.

Should the frontiers of another state lie so close to mine, that the crowing of the cocks and the barking of the dogs in the one, could be heard in the other, I would so arrange it, that the two peoples should arrive at old age, and die, without any intercourse having ever taken place between them.

CHAPTER LXXXI.

The language of Truth is not always elegant, whilst well-turned phrases often lack truth.

A Good man may not use choice words, but he who does so may not be good.

A Wise man may not be erudite, whilst he who is erudite may not be wise.

The Superior man does not garner up his knowledge, hence he is able to help others, and the more he gives out of his own store, the more there will remain.

The principle upon which Heaven acts, is to benefit all, and to injure none.

The principle upon which the Superior man acts, is to avoid being contentious.

THE END.

APPENDIX.

—o—

ON THE MEANING OF THE TITLE OF LÂO-TSZE'S BOOK—THE TÂO-TĬH-KING.

HAVING, for reasons which have been sufficiently stated in the preface, arrived at the conclusion, that the only satisfactory rendering of the character " *Tâo* " as used by Lâo-tsze is that of the word " *God*," the difficulties which have caused so much vexation of spirit and divergence of opinion amongst previous translators at once disappear ; and the second character " *tĭh* " readily lends itself to the rendering " *virtue of*," *i.e.*, " *nature of*," which I have adopted. But inasmuch as Lâo-tsze has not confined himself entirely to considerations connected with that one subject, but has mingled with them many reflections on the moral consequences which a knowledge of God must inevitably produce, I have thought it better to enlarge the somewhat meagre simplicity of the text, by the addition of a word " manifestations," so as to give the reader a clearer and more comprehensive idea of the subject matter which the old Chinese philosopher was endeavouring to enforce. Of course it is needless to make any reference to the third character, " *King*," which is only a term applied to all classical works. Neither do I think it necessary to enter into a criticism of the various translations of the title, which have hitherto been adopted by my predecessors.

CHAPTER I.

When the initial difficulty connected with the word " *Tâo* " has been disposed of, the text naturally lends itself to some such form of words as I have adopted.

In making an independent translation of the " *Tâo-tĭh-King*" my first object has been to seize upon the idea sought to be conveyed by Lâo-tsze, and then to find a form of words which would render it intelligible ; and this latter is no easy matter, for the style of the original is so meagre and abrupt, that the passages, with respect to words, are often little more than skeleton forms, which have to be elaborated and filled up in order to give them such an amount of coherence as will make them intelligible. I have endeavoured, however, whilst doing this, to preserve *as far as possible* the peculiar characteristics of the Chinese writer's style and diction.

CHAPTER II.

The portion I have treated metrically is also so rendered by v. Strauss.

CHAPTER III.

I have translated "*pûh tsăng*" by "*will not strive*" in the sense of " *will not emulate* "—approaching nearer to Dr Legge in this, than to either Stanislas Julien or v. Strauss.

CHAPTER IV.

The chief difficulty in this chapter proceeds from the opening sentence, " *Tâo ch'ung urh yung che.*" In chapter forty-five "*ch'ung*" is said to mean "*empty*," though that is only one of many meanings, and Dr Legge translates the passage :—" *The Tâo is (like) the emptiness of a vessel and in our employment of it. . . .*" and Stanislas Julien by :—" *Le Tâo est vide, si l'on en fait usage . . .*" and v. Strauss by :—*Tâo ist leer, und gebrauch er dess . . .*" But as I read the passage in connection with the context and the general scope and intention of the chapter, it becomes, literally :—" *God being unsubstantial made use of it*,"—referring evidently to the act of creation—"*and though we only have an imperfect knowledge of Him*, . . ." and so on to the end. The only change I have made has been to substitute "immaterial" for "*void*," "*empty*" or "unsubstantial," in order to bring the subject matter into harmony with that of preceding and following chapters.

It is worthy of remark that this is the only instance in which any allusion is made to the "Lord of Heaven;" and from the way it is introduced, there can be but little doubt that it was directed against the teaching of Confucius, for in the estimation of Lâo-tsze, that great Teacher, amongst other shortcomings, had been guilty of falling away from a belief in the Tâo—that is to say, in God—as professed in the earliest ages of mankind, and of accepting, as a substitution, the inferior conception of a corrupt age—" *the Lord of Heaven.*"

CHAPTER VI.

This chapter is given by the philosopher Lieh-Tsze (400 B.C.) as a quotation from Hwang-tih, and Dr Legge, in his indroduction to the "Texts of Tâoism," when referring to this, observes that the Chinese commentator Tû Tâo-kien (about A.D. 1300) remarks, in connection with this chapter, "that Lâo-tsze was accustomed to quote in his treatise passages from earlier records."

" *The Spirit of the Valley*" is evidently the creative energy of God, the productive exercise of which is referred to here, as well as in Chapter I., as an act of " Motherhood ;" consequently God the *Creator*, as formulated by Lâo-tsze, became not the " Father" of all things, as with us, but the " Mother," though the application of this term was confined within certain limits, for the masculine energies of his nature seem to have been equally recognised ; indeed it would have been impossible

for Lâo-tsze to have set aside the conviction that the action of
the male and female principles of nature—the "*Yang*" and
the "Yin"—was universal, and even extended in some mysterious way to the Great First Cause—the incomprehensible
"*Tâo.*"

CHAPTER X.

The obscurities which confessedly belong to this chapter, have
certainly not been diminished by the changes made in the text
by the Tâoist commentators, as will be seen by a reference to
the translations of Dr Legge, Stanislas Julien, and Victor v.
Strauss—all of whom have adopted them.

I have preferred to adhere to the original, and though my
rendering of the opening sentences might be modified, I believe
any change would be more in the direction of the arrangement
of the words, than in the meaning.

"The opening and shutting of the portals of heaven" is
evidently a figure of speech, which I have rendered by "the
processes of nature ;" and the remarkable simile of the "brood
hen" would lose all point and meaning were she not made
the subject of the succeeding sentences. Indeed, without this
treatment, the object Lâo-tsze had in view, which was to enforce
the doctrine of "inaction," or more strictly speaking of "non-
interference," is entirely lost, and we should be without the key
to much that would be otherwise incomprehensible in other
portions of his work.

It is evident that Lâo-tsze was always endeavouring—strug-
gling would be the better word—to be as explanatory and clear
as possible, whilst his commentators were never weary of finding
some occult meaning in his most simple words.

CHAPTER XIV.

The three characters which I have translated by "*invisible*,"
"*inaudible*," and "*intangible*," are the ones which v. Strauss—
following Remusat—considers to be a Chinese rendering of

three of the letters comprised in the Hebrew word Jehovah. Neither Dr Legge nor Stanislas Julien accept this view, and I think their arguments against it are conclusive·

CHAPTER XV.

This is evidently a continuation of the preceding chapter. In translating *"hwan"* by "self-effacement," I have followed Stanislas Julien. In other cases where I have differed from my predecessors, I have been governed in the choice of words by the necessities of the context. The dictionaries often give a large number of very diverse meanings, and the great difficulty a translator has to deal with is to know which one is most applicable—that is to say, best fulfils the conditions of the subject he has in hand. The meaning of the original has not only to be carefully preseved, but it has to be transmuted into the best idiomatic English the translator is capable of presenting it in. ˙

CHAPTER XVI.

See p. 96 of "Confucius, the Great Teacher." I have retained this metrical version as best conveying the meaning and character of the original.

CHAPTER XVII.

The key to the opening sentences of this chapter, is to be found in the closing paragraph of the preceeding one, of which it is evidently a continuation. In the second sentence—" *hĕa chi yŭ che*"—Dr Legge has substituted the negative "*pŭh*" for " *hĕa*," observing that "it does not affect the meaning of the passage," but as I read it, it does so very materially, by not only altering its whole tenour, but by preventing the chapter itself from being brought into harmony with the three following ones, to which it may be considered as the introduction.

CHAPTER XX.

I have adhered as closely to the text as possible, though I have not always succeeded in bringing my version into absolute agreement, with the work of my predecessors ; but the difference is only in detail.

CHAPTER XXI.

I have given this chapter as it appeared in " Confucius, the Great Teacher," as I found after many trials that I was unable to better it.

CHAPTER XXII.

I have followed v. Strauss in treating the opening sentences of this chapter as a quotation. Dr Legge does not, though he refers to them, in accordance with the original, as quoted, in his closing paragraph.

The chief difficulty is connected with the two last lines of the quotation—

" Shao⁻tsih tĭh
To tsih hwŏ."

Dr Legge, in agreement with Stanislas Julien, interpolates " desires " and translates—" He whose (desires) are few gets them ; he whose (desires) are many goes astray." Stanislas Julien — " Avec peu (de desirs) on acquiert le Tâo ; avec beaucoup (de desirs) on s'égare." Victor v. Strauss—" wenn wenig, so werd'erreicht ; wenn viel, so werde verfehlt." But none of these renderings appear to me to fulfil the necessary conditions, which are demanded by the application of the quotation in question, to the action of the Sage. I have endeavoured to do this without departing from verbal accuracy.

CHAPTER XXIII.

Dr Legge translates the opening sentence—" *He-jên tsze-jen* " —by " abstaining from speech marks him who is obeying the spontaneity of his nature." Stanislas Julien by—"celui qui ne parle pas (arrive au) non agir. V. Strauss by—"wenig reden ist naturgemäss." In each case the rendering of Chinese commentators having been followed. But the reading I have adopted for this passage is so natural, and so close to the original, that I can find no good reason for discarding it ; indeed I have been impressed most strongly with the feeling, that in every case Lâo-tsze—however he may have failed—endeavoured to be as clear and lucid as possible, and that in no instance is the difficulty of translation attributable to his having either sought to convey, or to conceal, by the use of mystic terms, occult ideas only capable of being comprehended by the initiated.

CHAPTER XXV.

I have adhered very closely to the version of this chapter which appeared in "Confucius, the Great Teacher." My rendering of the opening sentences is based upon the translation given of them both in Medhurst's and Morrison's dictionaries under the character "*hwan*," "things were confusedly mixed before Heaven and Earth were." I must confess to my version approaching nearer to a paraphrase than a literal translation, but I have, not the less, endeavoured to convey the *meaning* as accurately as possible, whilst preserving so far as was in my power the peculiar style belonging to the text.

Of all the chapters in this work, this is one of the most interesting and remarkable.

CHAPTER XXVII.

I have followed S. Julien in translating "*shih-ming*" as "doubly enlightened," which seems to agree best with the dictionary meaning given to "*shih*." In translating "*chê*" by "a knowledge of what is suitable," I have again followed the dictionary. The last passage, which Dr Legge renders, "This is called ' The utmost degree of mystery,'" has assumed the form which I have given it, from the meaning which is attached to " *Yaou* "—" an abstract of the most important "—in Morrison's dictionary.

CHAPTER XXVIII.

I have followed the example of both Dr Legge and v. Strauss in rendering this chapter metrically.

CHAPTER XXXI.

The pacific tone of this chapter is very remarkable ; but it is in accordance with the teaching, which in the course of ages, made the Chinese the least warlike, and the most peace-loving people in the world.

CHAPTER XXXIII.

The passage which I have rendered "he who dies and is not forgotten will be immortal " Dr Legge translates—" he who dies and does not perish will have longevity," in agreement with S. Julien. But—" is not forgotten " is as literal as "does not perish," and under the conditions in which " *Show* " is used it seems to me that " immortality " best conveys its meaning.

CHAPTER XXXVI.

The dictionary meaning of " *hëih*," which I have translated " to contract," is given as " to snuff up the nose," " to draw in the breath," but as " *chang* " lends itself most readily to the sense I have given it, I have thought it better to bring the two words into agreement by sacrificing a small amount of literal accuracy. " *Wei ming*," " the lustre of the moon," is evidently used metaphorically for " obscurely," " faintly," &c., and it is thus I have used it.

CHAPTER XXXVII.

In the opening sentence I have translated " *woo-wei* " by " rest," but am not satisfied with it, and yet " inaction," which would be more accurate, hardly gives a better meaning. Dr Legge adopts "does nothing (for the sake of doing it)," which is open to criticism. In many cases it evidently means "non-interference," in others "influence" as opposed to active effort. Perhaps in the present instance "quiescent" might be the best word. Again, "simplicity" might be taken exception to as the equivalent of "*Pŏ*," but it is extremely difficult to find anything better.

CHAPTER XXXVIII.

This, the first chapter of the second book, has to be read in connection with the eighteenth chapter, but even then it is very difficult to get a clear idea of Lâo-tsze's meaning. Dr Legge and Stanislas Julien give a personal application to what he says, but v. Strauss does not, and I have followed his example. It is very puzzling to know when "*tĭh*" is to be treated as a Divine attribute, and when it is to be taken as a moral virtue. Lâo-tsze himself does not always seem to have made up his mind about it, and it is at times almost impossible to find out the exact meaning he attached to "*e-wei*," "*yŭ-e-wei*," and *woo-e-wei*," for it would produce the wildest confusion were they always to be translated by the same terms.

CHAPTER XXXIX.

I have translated the character "*yu*" in the last paragraph by "a foundation," which is one of the meanings given in Medhurst's dictionary.

CHAPTER XL.

Perhaps the most correct translation of the opposites "*yew*" and "*woŏ*" would be existent and non-"existent," but as used in this chapter, it is difficult to avoid rendering them as I have done, which also brings them in harmony with the mode of treatment adopted in the first chapter.

CHAPTER XLI.

Victor v. Strauss extends the metrical quotation to the end of this chapter, but Dr Legge excludes the last two sentences ; he, too, renders the rest metrically. I had at first followed his example, but the oftener I read this chapter over, the more I became convinced that the verses cited as written by the "phrase" or "sentence makers," were confined to the limits I have given them, for although the following lines have the same metrical construction, the ideas conveyed in them are so entirely those of Lâo-tsze, that to have accepted them as having been put forward by another, would go a long way towards placing him in a secondary position, and almost reduce him to the condition of a plagiarist ; and I selected prose for this latter portion as conveying far more closely and clearly the meaning of the original. In order to prove how much it would have lost in force, I give my metrical version for comparison :—

> As a vast space
> Whose bounds evade the sight,
> As a crude vase
> Which ever grows in height,
> As a deep voice
> From which rare words escape,
> As a huge figure
> Void, and free from shape,
> So stands before us
> He who has no name,
> The mystic cause
> From whence all goodness came.

CHAPTER XLII.

This is the chapter which led some of its first translators to the conclusion that Lâo-tsze had a knowledge of a triune God.

But even amongst those who did not share this opinion, there exists a wide difference as to the exact meaning belonging to the opening sentences. I do not pretend to be able to present a solution of the difficulties by which the subject is surrounded, or to adjudicate between the different commentators who have dealt with it, preferring to set forth the text as I find it. Though I must confess to seeing no reason why the opening paragraph should mean more than a reference to the evolution of the first created unit, through the employment of the natural energy of the Great First Cause, into an infinite variety of forms.

The passages which I have translated by " He who humbleth shall be exalted" and " He who exalteth shall be humbled," could, of course, if taken by themselves, have been rendered, word for word, by—" Things may either, through making themselves small, become great, or by making themselves great, become small," but they have to be brought into agreement with what precedes, the keynote of which is to be found in the latter portion of chapter xxxix.

I have translated "*K'hëäng lëang chay puh tih ke sze*" by " no opposition or obstruction can destroy it," which is sufficiently near, for literally it would be, " Violent obstruction would be unable to obtain its death," whilst it completes the meaning of a chapter which has, in my opinion, been made unnecessarily obscure.

CHAPTER XLV.

Both Dr Legge and v. Strauss translate this chapter metrically. I endeavoured to follow suit, but found I could not keep sufficiently close to the text to give a clear idea of its meaning, so I gave it up.

CHAPTER XLVIII.

In my translation of the second sentence I have followed S. Julien.

CHAPTER XLIX.

In the second paragraph Dr Legge substitutes "*tĭh*," to "obtain," for "*tĭh*," "virtue," and I have adopted his reading, though I am not quite sure that the latter might not be used as a verb in the sense of "to make a virtue of." My translation of the closing paragraph is most in agreement with that of Victor v. Strauss.

CHAPTER L.

The commentators have done their best to make this chapter hopelessly obscure. My version comes nearest to that of v. Strauss.

CHAPTER LII.

Had I been more literal, my version would have commenced in some such way as this :—" In the beginning of the world God manifests Himself as its Mother, and it was not until the world had obtained a Mother that it became possible to gain a knowledge of that Mother's offspring. But it is only through the knowledge of the offspring that we are enabled to restore and preserve a knowledge of the Mother, and he who is . . ." and so on.

I have taken the phrase, "*Sih kh'e t'huy pĕ kh'e mun*" figuratively, for I believe it to have been used in that sense, and I have translated "*jow*," which has the meaning of "plants and trees just budding forth," as well as that of "flexible," "pliant," "still," and "quiet," by—"the germs of vital energy," which, though it may not *quite* give the idea sought to be conveyed, is something very like it.

Dr Legge has translated the last paragraph metrically, but v. Strauss has not. The latter renders the closing sentence, "*Shi wei shĭh ch'hang*," much as I do.

CHAPTER LIII.

As used in the beginning of this chapter, the character "*Tâo*" is evidently used for the "Path" or "Way," meaning, of course,

" God's path," " God's way," but in the last sentence it seems to me best rendered by the form of words I have adopted.

CHAPTER LIV.

Neither Dr Legge or v. Strauss treat the same portions metrically ; some portions lend themselves more readily to metrical treatment than others, and by this the translator's choice is often guided. I cannot, however, conceal the fact, that under the exigences of rhyme, it is all but impossible to keep close to the original.

CHAPTER LV.

This is a very peculiar chapter, and it would be impossible to translate some of the passages in the same terse, outspoken language which belongs to the original ; though I have equally preserved the idea contained in them. Without the introductory " which fears neither " the comparison with the new-born babe appears meaningless, and in this I have followed S. Julien. In the opening sentences Dr Legge and v. Strauss are at variance.

CHAPTER LVI.

As in chapter lvii. I have treated the passage " *Sih kh'e t'huy pe kh'e mun*" as figurative ; when translated literally it becomes very unmanageable.

CHAPTER LVII.

I have translated "*Ching*" by "justice," but "straightforwardness" would be more exact, and probably the better word.

CHAPTER LIX.

By substituting "*füh*," to "return," for "*füh*," to "use," to "employ," to "cause to be done," &c., Dr Legge has completely altered the meaning of the second paragraph. I have not attempted a line by line translation, but after much careful examination, I could not find my way to a more accurate rendering of the text, as a whole, than the form of words I have adopted.

CHAPTER LXII.

I think this chapter shows more conclusively than any other, the necessity of translating the word " *Tâo*," as generally used by Lâo-tsze, by God.

CHAPTER LXIII.

This chapter is obviously a continuation of the preceding one, hence my treatment of it.

CHAPTER LXIV.

My rendering of the last three sentences differs from that of Dr Legge; but then I read it literally " To repeat the fault which is committed by the mass of mankind of assisting the natural processes (or self-development) of nature, (is that) which he dares not do ; " and this accords with what has previously been said on the same subject.

CHAPTER LXV.

I have treated the concluding paragraph as impersonal : it being, as I read it, a record of the impressions which were produced on Lâo-tsze's mind by a sense of failure, for it will have been observed that he often endeavours to veil his own want of clearness by bringing it into contrast with the impenetrable obscurity which surrounds his great central idea—the mystery of God.

CHAPTER LXVII.

Dr Legge, in accordance with the views of several Chinese commentators, translates the fifth character in the first sentence —the ordinary meaning of which is the personal pronoun " I " —by " my Tâo," but I have preferred to follow S. Julien and v. Strauss.

I have interpolated the definition of " love," according to the sense in which the word was employed by Lâo-tsze in this chapter. Perhaps " affection " would have been a better word : Dr Legge translates—"tenderness."

CHAPTER LXVIII.

Dr Legge translates this chapter metrically, but v. Strauss does not, and I have followed his example.

CHAPTER LXIX.

The literal translation of the sentence " *Ho muh ta yü king t'heih* " is "there is no greater misfortune than to esteem an adversary lightly," and this is the sense in which I have rendered the passage. I have rendered " *Gae* " in the last sentence by " love," in the same sense as that in which it was used in chapter lxvii.; for the other meanings, such as " pity " or " compassion," are scarcely applicable to the conditions of the text.

CHAPTER LXXII.

A great diversity of opinion exists as to the terms in which this chapter should be translated. I have been satisfied with giving the general idea which Lâo-tsze was seeking to convey, but cannot pretend to literal accuracy.

I

CHAPTER LXXIII.

In my translation of this chapter I have adhered as closely as possible to the text, treating the several passages as detached thoughts jotted down as they occurred to the writer, though they always stand in a certain relation to each other. I have followed v. Strauss in rendering the last paragraph metrically, and as a quotation, though the last point is rather doubtful.

CHAPTER LXXIV.

Dr Legge translates " *Chang yü tze shā chay sha* " by "there is always One who presides over the infliction of death ; " v. Strauss by — " Immerdar giebts einen Blutrichter, der da todtet ; " and S. Julien by—" Il-y-a constamment un magistrat suprême qui inflige la mort."

CHAPTER LXXVI.

Although in the closing sentences the same word " K'heang " is applied to both an army and a tree, it is evident that they cannot be translated by identical terms in both cases.

CHAPTER LXXVIII.

Here I again find myself at variance with my predecessors. Dr Legge translates the quotation at the end of the chapter metrically, and his rendering is very different from mine. The first sentence in it—" *show kwo che kow* "—means literally "to receive the kingdom's filth, and " *shày-tseih* " has the meaning of the " spirits of the fields and grain." In like manner I read " *show kwo che pǔh tseang* " " the misery of the State," so that word for word the quotation would be—

" The receiver of the nation's filth is called the spirit of the land and corn ;
The receiver of the nation's misery is called its king."

But such an enlargement of the text as I have given it is clearly needed to make it comprehensible.

CHAPTER LXXX.

The reading I have adopted seems the most natural construction to put on the passage "*She yü shih pih che k'hc urh pŭh yung*" : it is most in agreement with S. Julien.

CHAPTER LXXXI.

It is very difficult to do justice to the natural simplicity of style which belongs to this chapter. I have endeavoured to adhere as closely to the text as possible, but in this chapter, as in many others, I fear I have not always been successful in finding the most suitable form of words, but in the words of Lâo-tsze, "well-turned phrases often lack truth."

PRINTED BY
TURNBULL AND SPEARS
EDINBURGH.